John Russell Fearn was on
science fiction, who, at hi
producing material under
revival of interest in this e
his best in CONQUEST C

John Russell Fearn

Conquest of the Amazon

Futura Publications Limited
An Orbit book

An Orbit book

First published in Great Britain in 1973
in the Cosmos Science Fiction series

First Futura Publications edition 1976

ISBN 0 8600 7858 2
Printed in Great Britain by
Hazell Watson & Viney Ltd
Aylesbury, Bucks

Futura Publications Limited
110 Warner Road
Camberwell, London SE5

The Golden Amazon first made her appearance in FANTASTIC ADVENTURES, for July, 1939, in a 10,000 word story – which incidentally won the 75 dollars prize over Edgar Rice Burroughs' THE SCIENTISTS REVOLT. After that the Amazon appeared in three more novelettes, and then faded out when I quit writing for the American magazines in 1943. But throughout the war years the idea remained that she was too good to lose, so I decided to make a full-length book about her....

In the original short stories she was lost on Venus as a baby, and the Venusian climate turned her into a superwoman: in the first novel about her, published by World's Work in April, 1944, she was a baby lost in the Blitz, operated upon by a super-surgeon. He changed her glandular structure which – at maturity – would mean she would have more than human strength, abnormally brilliant intelligence, and an almost sexless outlook on life. The surgeon's idea was that she would lead the world to eternal peace; but he miscalculated and her incredible knowledge of science practically led her to destroy the world by her finding of atomic power (prior, be it noted, to the actual discovery of the atomic bomb.) In this novel she also discovered synthesis, including how to make an exact image of herself, and by this means she escaped punishment as the world, seeing 'her' die, assumed she was done for. Actually it was her synthetic image which died. This paved the way for THE GOLDEN AMAZON RETURNS.

THE GOLDEN AMAZON, however, attracted the attention of *Toronto Star* when it was submitted to them and they published it also, in the March 25th 1945 issue, as the novel of the week. Since that time every adventure of the Amazon has been published first by them, and the British version by World's Work. But World's Work, unfortunately, had more paper trouble than *Toronto Star*, which explains why the latter had published the sixth adventure by the time the second book was being issued.

With THE GOLDEN AMAZON RETURNS, which concerned itself with V–2 attack and atomic power, as it well might be in the future, the superwoman seemed to settle down into a routine job, namely, the advancement of Earth's scientific culture on the one hand, and the routing of menaces, physical and scientific, on the other. She changed her tactics also – realizing she was biting off too much in trying to rule the world she instead decided to fight on the side of the law. She became a kind of super female Robin Hood, with scientific trimmings, outwitting every kind of public menace from shady financiers to master-scientists.

With this novel came the beginnings of space travel which were carried a stage further in THE GOLDEN AMAZON'S TRIUMPH, wherein the conquest of Venus was attempted, to a great extent successfully. Much business was left unfinished however, and a Venusian menace returned in THE AMAZON'S DIAMOND QUEST, said menace being effectually routed this time. In fact, it was not the main plot; this consisted of the discovery of a cavern of pure diamonds (created by volcanic action) which the Amazon had to protect from thieves both Venusian and Earthly. In her travels she routed the Chameleon Men of Venus – who could assume any form at will which made her job difficult – and turned over the diamond cavern to the Earth authorities.

Now that Venus is safely in the bag and a space line established (not by the Amazon who is a lone wolf, but by her friends of the early days) the Amazon can apparently relax somewhat. But she finds that the menace of the earlier stories, Carl Mueller, had a daughter who, now grown up, proves as big a nuisance as her father. So in THE AMAZON STRIKES AGAIN, the Amazon sets off to deal with this scientific young woman, and her adventures carry her from a subtropical basin at the South Pole to the planet Venus once again, in the course of which the Earth is in danger of destruction from synthetically-created tornadoes. Here, on Venus, the menace angle is finished completely and Venus is out of the picture – now a safe colony of Earth.

Pursuing her ideal to make the whole solar system one Union of the Universe the Amazon next set out to conquer Mars – with a race of 5,000 highly-scientific Martians – to bring the apparently empty planet next in line as an Earth colony. But the Martians have similar aspirations for the Earth. The upshot is – after the Amazon is duplicated by the Martian Controllix and the Earth nearly brought to ruin because of it – that the last of the Martian armadas are tricked by the Amazon into being hurled into the sun. This leaves Mars as an empty world to be taken over.

But the atomic power motors of the space machine which have been flung into the sun have a detrimental effect on the sun itself. This is the main theme of CONQUEST OF THE AMAZON. In this yarn the Amazon – with a new character, Abna of Atlantis – fights this time to restore the monarch of the heavens to his former glory, and at the same time has to live down the blame for causing the trouble. . . .

And so it goes on – Jupiter, Saturn, Uranus, Neptune, Pluto – and beyond. With a woman like the Amazon anything can – and probably will – happen!

John Russell Fearn

Blackpool, Lancs.
2nd November, 1948.

CHAPTER I

Morris Arnside, autocratic chief of the World Food Combine, could not quite believe the figures he was studying. Had the year been 1972 he could easily have thought that statisticians had erred in their calculations, or perhaps that there was some double-dealing going on somewhere – but in this year of 2032 there was no room for doubt. Men racked their brains no more with calculations. Flawless machines computed everything to the last fraction, and they never made a mistake – for which reason the report was all the more mystifying.

'Beyond me,' Arnside confessed to himself.

For a moment or two he sat gazing out of the window. Light snow was falling, driven by flurries of bitter wind. It might have been mid-January instead of late May – but then it had been intensely cold for six months and more.

Finally Arnside pressed a button on his desk and his chief assistant and deputy food controller entered.

'Good morning Mr. Arnside,' he greeted – and Arnside glared at him with prominent grey eyes.

'I'll be hanged if it is! Sit down, Mathers. There's something I want to talk over with you.'

The assistant settled in the chair at the opposite side of the desk and waited. For Morris Arnside to be short-tempered was nothing new. He lived well, ate heartily, took little exercise, and was always volcanic in consequence. But for him to be anxious was definitely unusual.

'I've just had the reports for the first three months of this year,' Arnside said at length. 'They're staggering! Crops and staple foods are nearly 80 per cent below the normal yield. If things go on at this rate there won't be enough to feed the world's population by the end of the year, and that means we'll have to fall back on synthetic products, something which the majority of people hate.'

'Yes, sir,' Mathers agreed imperturbably.

'I've been trying to think of some reason for this tremendous falling off,' Arnside added, his fleshy jowls wagging with the emphasis of his words. 'I'll be hanged if I can, though. What has happened to our own British agriculture, the Canadian wheat fields, the United States grain-growing areas? All of them are just dying, man! Dying!'

'It has puzzled me,' Mathers responded. 'The reports are similar from all sources. The seasons are said to be changing. Take today, for instance, and we're right in the middle of spring. Snowing fast, and looks likely to continue. And the temperature hasn't risen much over freezing point since December of last year. I have been gathering weather reports from all over the world recently, and in every case there is a marked decline in mean temperatures – even in the tropics. Crops, in consequence are far behind normal.'

'The members of the combine must be made to produce 80 per cent more than they usually do,' Arnside decided. 'If they don't there'll be a penalty, and I'll issue a directive to that effect. It's the only way. Laziness, that's what it is! Living in a world of plenty, they think they can relax. They can't – and most certainly they're not going to make an unusually cold spring the excuse. I'll settle it!'

'Yes, sir,' Mathers murmured.

'It would help,' Arnside added, 'if you showed a little more enthusiasm.'

'I'm afraid I can't, sir. I think I know what we are fighting, and it rather terrifies me.'

The food controller stared. 'A slowing up in crop production terrifies you? Don't be an idiot, man!'

Mathers knew his chief far too well to take offence at his brusqueness. 'I have been studying this business pretty thoroughly – not entirely for professional reasons, but because I'm naturally curious. I may be wrong, but I don't think we'll ever get the crops to rights again. And I don't think we'll ever get warm weather again, either.'

'Do you mind telling me what on earth you're talking about?' Arnside demanded.

Mathers rose and went to the immense window. He stood gazing out over the fantastically lofty roofs of 2032 London; then he turned and motioned his superior. Arnside joined him and they stood gazing through the whirling snow into the grey sky.

'Well?' Arnside asked bluntly.

'Through the cloud breaks, sir, you can see the sun,' Mathers said, pointing. 'There – practically overhead at this hour.'

Arnside peered diagonally through the glass. 'Yes, I see it,' he acknowledged. 'Look pretty yellow, too. Morc like a foggy sun than a spring one. Mist intervening, I suppose.'

'Partly,' Mathers acknowledged, 'but look at the sun itself. What do you notice about it?'

Arnside did not think it strange at that moment that he could gaze at the sun without difficulty. It hurt the eye no more than if seen through dense orange-tinted glass. Curious for it to be so dim in late spring. For some moments he stared, then clouds drifted across and hid the view.

'It looks a bit speckled,' he decided. 'Rather like a pudding into which somebody has spattered currants.'

'An apt simile, sir,' Mathers observed. 'Sun spots.'

The food controller thumped the window frame. 'Look here, Mathers, talk sense, will you? What have sun spots got to do with it? There have been sun spots ever since – well, ever since the sun came into being, I suppose. They cause trouble, sure – such as radio interference, thunderstorms, and so forth, but they can't interfere with crops, surely?'

'Not directly, sir, but I think that an excess of them is causing the cool weather. The sun has not been free of spots for the last two years. I know, because I'm an amateur astronomer and I'm interested in such things. The average citizen hardly seems to know what a sun spot looks like, and he certainly doesn't study them. It's extraordinary for sun spots to keep on growing on the sun's disc. They usually abate after their normal cycle is complete. This time they haven't.'

There was something tremendously wrong up there in the bleak grey sky, Arnside realized. He knew Mathers intimately. He was a cold-blooded, youngish man, a clever scientist in his way, and certainly not given to exaggeration.

Arnside groped for words. 'Are you telling me that the sun's gone haywire or something?'

'There is that possibility,' Mathers replied. 'It is as prone to disorder and death as any other sentient thing. Scientists are perfectly aware that the sun must die some day from some cause or other, and I have the uneasy feeling that that day may not be far distant.'

This time Arnside did not say anything. The situation was too preposterous to grasp.

'Only one person or group of persons can solve this,' he said at last. 'The astronomers. And if they have been withholding vital information I'll tell them publicly exactly what I think about them! Book me a reservation on the next helicoliner following the Mount Everest route. I'm going to find out what Dr. Standish has to say.'

Dr. Luke Standish was the astronomer-in-chief of Everest Observatory, that lofty eminence built in 1990 and jointly controlled by every nation on the Earth. Here, above the clouds, surrounded by scientific appliances, which brought a tempered warmth to the former climbers' paradise, the spare, middle-aged Standish with his quiet voice and profound thinking kept a constant watch on the heavens, pooling the information supplied him by his own army of assistants and from the other observatories scattered about the world.

With space travel as common as flying, the presence of any danger in outer space was his responsibility. Thousands might die if he made one miscalculation upon a flying meteor or deadly cosmic gas area.

He confessed to a certain inner surprise when from his office he saw the London–Tibet helicoliner detouring from its normal course to land in the observatory grounds. He was even more surprised when only one passenger alighted, and almost immediately he recognized the heavy figure and blunt features of the food controller.

When Arnside had been shown into the office, Dr. Standish said: 'Unexpected pleasure. Have a seat.' And glancing through the window he added: 'I take it you are not returning immediately, since you have permitted the liner to continue its journey?'

'I expect to be here quite a few hours,' Arnside replied. 'I'm going to dig for information – lots of it! My job and maybe the fate of the world's population may depend on how much you can tell me.'

'Indeed? What's the trouble?'

'What in blazes is the matter with the sun?'

'You have anticipated me by a few days,' Standish remarked. 'I was – and still am – intending to make an announcement after consultation with the various officials responsible for the world's well-being . . . Yourself included, of course.'

CHAPTER II

Arnside said: 'Dr. Standish, my assistant – a keen amateur astronomer – tells me that the sun is going crazy or something. That it has spots longer than it should have. Now, I'm a commercial man. But even I can't help but notice that the sun looks queer. What do you think is going to happen?'

'I think,' Standish answered, 'that we are witnessing the death of a monarch, and the inevitable end of the world.'

The food controller sat motionless.

Standish went on: 'You must be aware of the lowering temperature all over the world? Even the tropical regions are chilly compared to what they should be.'

'That I know. I'm here because crops are failing and I've got to find out why.'

'I'm afraid there is nothing you can do – except provide synthetic foods. I have withheld the facts for as long as possible to be sure that there's no possibility of a mistake. Now I am forced to the staggering truth. The sun is dying. One might call it a solar cancer.' The astronomer got to his feet. 'Come with me, controller, and let me explain in more detail. You will merely have a preview of what all the world will have to know shortly.'

Arnside rose and followed Standish through an adjoining doorway and into the filing-room. Standish took some pictures from a cabinet.

'These,' he said, as the food controller looked on, 'are spectro-heliograph plates of the sun taken since late 2030. You wish me to be as untechnical as possible, of course?'

'Yes, I'm a practical man.'

'Well, then, normally sun-spot cycles reach a certain maximum and then fade out. These show the beginning of the present cycle in 2030.'

Standish laid down a series of plates. The sun was flawlessly photographed with two irregular marks on the centre of his disc.

Standish continued: '2031, and the plates showed as many as six sun spots with the two original ones vastly enlarged. And this was taken two days ago,' Standish finished.

Arnside stared at the final plate with a queer feeling at his heart. The sun was visible as a circle, but all over his face were mottled holes and chasms, infinitely more of them than the naked eye could see. The sun looked like a football spattered with mud.

'Never before,' the astronomer resumed, 'have sun spots spread to the solar poles, where they are now. Instead of passing away after their normal cycle they have gone on multiplying.' A shade of emotion quavered his voice. 'Imagine our feelings when we saw this happening – when we could watch it in a movie film photographed day by day. The death pangs of the lord of day and—'

Arnside interrupted impatiently. 'What's the cause of it? Can't we stop it? We've got space travel. We can reach the sun if we want—'

'And do what?' Standish shook his head. 'The explanation is scientific, Mr. Arnside, and perfectly in accord with astronomical law. There are two types of stars in the universe – main sequence or red stars and white dwarfs. Our sun is a main-sequence star with a stellar absolute magnitude of 4·85. The absolute magnitude is between 4·88 and 3·54. Therefore, our sun being at 4·85 was dangerously near the line of instability. You follow me?'

'What's that got to do with his spots?'

'The internal temperature of our sun was about 32,000,000 degrees when it was normal. It was a star in which the atoms were still surrounded by the K-rings of electrons, while the exterior rings had been stripped away by the tremendous heat. But any substantial rise in the internal temperature of the sun would cause the atoms to no longer exist as such. There'd only be free electrons and stripped nuclei. The star would rapidly become unstable and gradually move on to the next state of instability – that of the white dwarf.'

'And what would that mean – in plain language.'

'That the sun would never again recover his radiation. It

would become small and useless – like the Companion of Sirus.'

The astronomer seemed impossibly calm considering what he was saying. Nor had he finished. He continued quietly:

'Something – we are not certain what – caused the sun's internal temperature to become enormously increased for a brief time. It coincided with an abnormal number of spots. The spots, with their cooling blanket, kept in the sun's internal heat and the atoms were stripped. It was, in effect a vast cave-in, of which the sun spots are the outward sign. Finally the sun's photosphere will collapse and the white dwarf stage will then have been reached. Some of those sun spots are even now tens of thousands of miles across.'

Arnside gazed up again through the window on the yellow orb. It looked a mockery as it hung there, blotched and ugly. About it, stars were faintly visible in the violet-tinged heaven. Arnside's own thoughts of a holiday in Florida under blue skies upon sun-drenched beaches suddenly underwent a drastic revision. With difficulty he found words.

'There's – no possibility of a mistake?'

'I wish there were.' The astronomer returned the file to its cabinet and stood with hands in pockets, musing. 'It is for the government of the World Council to decide what shall be done. As I see it, there are two alternatives facing the human race. One is to go underground and there be prepared to spend the rest of its life until Earth crumbles away with age – or to somehow create another sun.' He shook his head and smiled wanly. 'Great though our science is, it is not great enough for that.'

The first shock having abated somewhat, Arnside stood musing. Then presently he spoke:

'Doctor, there must be some reason why the sun increased its internal temperature as it did. It just couldn't do it in the ordinary way, could it?'

'It could, but it is most unlikely,' Standish responded. 'Stray matter in space, drawn into the sun and exploded atomically by the teriffic heat might have caused it.'

The food controller said: 'Two years ago an armada of Martian space machines – flying saucers as they were called – were hurled into the sun and destroyed. There were atomic power plants in those machines. Would not that armada and the exploding atomic force plants set up a vast solar disturbance?'

'There, I think, you have the answer,' Standish admitted. 'It occurred to me long ago, and the time of the disturbance's commencement dates from when that armada fell in the sun, hurled there by the Golden Amazon. Whatever the initial cause we have to face the consequences.'

'You mean the Golden Amazon has,' Arnside snapped. 'If she hadn't caused that armada to be flung into the sun it wouldn't be dying now! That makes her directly responsible!'

'But unwittingly,' the astronomer protested. 'She risked her life to destroy that armada. It saved the world from horrible invasion and opened up Mars as a colony for Earth – as Venus is. It would be preposterous to accuse the Amazon of being the cause of our troubles.'

The food controller gave a grim smile. 'That's a matter of opinion, doctor. As a scientist you probably admire the Amazon because she is also a scientist. I am one of her enemies. I believe that back of her mind she has never had but one thought – to destroy this world of ours and all it contains. She tried it once with atomic power, remember – and failed. Why shouldn't she try it this way, masking her treachery under the cloak of bravery by destroying the Martians, potential enemies, at the same time?'

The astronomer gave a shrug. 'I have nothing but the frankest admiration for her. She is certainly the greatest scientist the world has ever known, and sometimes I wonder where we would have been without her. She gave us usable atomic power, space travel, colonization of other worlds, destroyed all menaces likely to afflict us.'

'She is still a dangerous woman with only one objective, doctor – to either master or destroy the people of this planet. Concerning this business with the sun. Have you asked her for an opinion?'

'It was the first thing I tried to do – over 18 mouths ago when the trouble first became apparent and I realized what was coming. Unfortunately she can't be located.'

The food controller thought for a while, then he said: 'With your permission, doctor, I will stay here for a day or so and take down all the necessary facts concerning this solar trouble so I can report to the World Council, and explain the crop failures. You, I assume, will support me later when you make your own statement?'

'Of course.' The astronomer moved to the door. 'Come this way, controller I am sure everything can be arranged for your comfort as long as you wish to stay.'

CHAPTER III

One evening some days later Morris Arnside called upon Brice Torrington, the metals king, at his Surrey residence. Though it was the first day of June, Arnside's ato-limousine wound its way between banks of snow which marked the drive of the Torrington house. The evening had darkened prematurely, as did all evenings now, the yellow globe hanging over the horizon dispensing hardly any light or heat.

Brice Torrington was in his library, expecting his visitor. Tall and lean, with a mouth like a spring trap, he was undisputed boss of world metals.

'I'm here for two reasons,' Arnside said. 'The present solar trouble – and the Golden Amazon. The end of the world is within sight. I thought you should know that. In a day or two Dr. Standish will be telling everybody about it.

'End of the world?' Torrington repeated, musing. 'From a materialist like you that's a remarkable statement.'

Arnside gave the facts as they had been given to him by Standish, but without the technical details. Torrington brooded as he listened, his eyes narrowed.

'There'll be a way around it,' he said finally.

'Standish is going to suggest deep shelters and under-world galleries when he addresses the council. According to him, the surface of the Earth will be uninhabitable in two years. By then every man, woman and child must be below ground, warmed and lighted by atomic power. You, as metals king, will naturally be called upon to supply the shelters. You'll make your already tremendous fortune six or seven times as large.'

'What else is on your mind?'

'The Golden Amazon. I think we have a chance at last to get rid of her – legally. I mean. She is as much your enemy as mine. Standish thinks that the Martian armada being thrown into the sun caused it to start decaying. That makes the Golden Amazon directly responsible. What is more significant is the fact that she cannot be found anywhere in this moment of deadly crisis when her scientific knowledge is so desperately needed. Doesn't it look as though she deliberately set out to ruin the sun, and then vanished? Doesn't it look like revenge on her part? She found that she could not control this world as she wanted, and apparently reversed her tactics and gave her knowledge freely to advance mankind – but I believe she has only been waiting for the supreme chance to hit back, and has done so.'

'Perhaps,' Torrington muttered.

Arnside said: 'If she remains absent we can convince the council that she's the cause of our troubles. We can insist that she be found, brought to trial, and then banished as a menace to society. We can be rid of her. Without her cold-blooded supervision, you could do much more. So could I. So could Swainson of Atomic Corporation, Ranleigh of Transport, and many others. We wouldn't get the Dodd Space Line behind us, of course, because the Dodds and Wilsons are indirectly related to the Amazon.'

Torrington said: 'To be rid of the Golden Amazon has been the ambition of my life. I'll call a conference at my office of Swainson, Ranleigh and others. We'll agree on a policy, and state it at the World Council when Standish makes his statement. In the meantime, let's hope the Amazon stops away and so blackens her case.'

While Arnside and Torrington were talking, the space liner Atom Cloud was landing at the spaceport, in central London, at the end of a journey from Venus. Aboard it, one of the 200 passengers, was Ethel Wilson, daughter of the controller of the Earth terminal of the Dodd Space Line.

She hurried through the customs, a slim, dark-headed, blue-eyed girl. In the administration building she took an elevator to the 20th floor.

Ethel hurried along the corridor to the door at the far end. She tapped lightly and entered. The grey-haired, heavy-shouldered man at the big desk glanced up in the glow of the cold-light globes in the ceiling.

'Rosy Cheeks!' he ejaculated, jumping to his feet. 'Am I glad to see you again.'

'Hello, dad.' The girl giggled affectionately as her father

embraced her. 'And please stop calling me Rosy Cheeks!'

'But they are!'

'In a wind like this, what else do you expect? It's my childhood name, though, and I am 28.'

Chris Wilson, head of the Earth Space Line terminal, smiled and drew up a chair for his daughter. When she was seated he stood surveying her.

'Grand to have you back,' he said. 'Your mother and I have missed you a lot. Have a good time with the Kerrigans on Venus?'

'Yes, but as I told you over the space-phone, I thought it was time I hopped back and discussed something with you. Something very important.'

'I've been looking forward to it ever since I got your message. Well, what is this important something? A boy friend?'

'No, dad. It's the sun.'

'The sun!' Wilson repeated. 'The only topic of conversation everywhere one goes.'

'What's happened to it?' Ethel broke in. 'On Venus, where the temperature rarely used to drop below 300 degrees, it's only 120. It has been like that for nearly a year now, and getting cooler all the time. I also noticed as we crossed space that the Martian ice caps extended halfway down to his equator now, whereas Earth is splotched all over with ice drifts. As for the sun we didn't even need the screens up during our voyage. His light's feeble, and his heat enormously decreased. Then there are those terrific dark marks all over him. What's happened, dad? Are we running into a spacial glacial epoch or something?'

'I've heard reports,' Chris Wilson answered slowly, 'to the effect that the sun is dying. All things die, even suns – but this has happened millions of years before science expected it.'

Ethel reflected. She did not appear frightened, as indeed she was not. She had been in too many tight corners to be easily scared.

'I sort of suspected something like that,' she said at last. 'I thought first-hand information on how space looks, and the condition on Venus, might help you and Aunt Vi. Naturally she is going to try to do something?'

His daughter's unswerving loyalty to the Golden Amazon – whom she called her Aunt Vi – was something which always made Chris Wilson smile.

'I don't doubt your Aunt Vi would do something if she were available,' Chris Wilson replied, 'but she isn't – and I can't locate her. For the past 18 months she's been missing – about the same length of time you've been away.'

'But she's got to be found,' Ethel said. 'The Earth is in danger of extinction – and in fact the whole solar system is if the sun should die. We can't fight a thing so vast by ourselves. Our science isn't up to it.'

Chris Wilson said nothing. There was nothing he could say. He and the Golden Amazon were friends – nothing more – and that only in the line of business. The Golden Amazon had no real affection for anybody, unless it were for Ethel. Risking the Amazon's anger in an attempt to locate her was more than Chris Wilson dared do.

Ethel resumed. 'She came back to Earth after destroying that Martian armada which fell into the sun; then she made arrangements for Mars to be reinhabited and provided with oceans and breathable atmosphere. After that I went to Venus to stay with the Kerrigans—'

'And your Aunt Vi told me she was going to be busy,' her father put in. 'I haven't seen her since – 18 months ago.'

'Surely, before things get really bad, she'll turn up and help us?'

'I sincerely hope so.'

'If Aunt Vi doesn't come back, what is going to be done?'

'I don't know. Man always survives. We might go underground. The World Council is meeting tomorrow to make a statement. I've made private plans. We're giving up our London residence and going to Brazil. There's still warmth there, enough to keep us comfortable for maybe a year. England is impossible to live in these days.'

Ethel had no particular wish to go to Brazil. Her father had maintained a residence there for some years, chiefly for the use of the Amazon when she required it, for her researches often took her to the tropics. But the place was lonely, miles from anywhere, on the very edge of the trackless forest.

She said: 'I hope nothing's happened to Aunt Vi. She takes such fantastic risks sometimes. What can she be doing, I wonder?'

Her father reached for his hat and coat. 'No use conjecturing, I'm afraid. Let's get along and give your mother a pleasant surprise. She's aching to have you back home. Tomorrow we'll see what the council has to say. I have to attend it. You might as well come too.'

CHAPTER IV

On the following day there was little change in the weather. The sky was grey, the wind biting, the daylight dim. Chris Wilson and Ethel found their car held up at times by traffic blocks and snow-drifts as they were driven to the World Council meeting in the centre of the city; then upon entering the great edifice they partly forgot the external discomfort in the midst of the light and warmth which greeted them.

In the assembly hall, its huge cupola of roof lined with batteries of cameras and television transmitters, were gathered delegates from every land, all of them members of the World Council, the elected body of the people of Earth whose duty it was to rule, extending the same justice and protection to all races and creeds.

Chris Wilson took his place, Ethel beside him, and waited. He recognized scientists, engineers, commercial giants, astronomers – every type and profession. Then he turned his attention to the rostrum as President Vancourt, head of the World Council, rose to speak.

'My friends . . .' His voice was steady but filled with a definite air of sombreness. 'We are here today to listen to a statement by Dr. Standish, our chief astronomer – a statement of such profound significance that I beg you to listen to every word without interruption. It concerns the strange condition of the sun. Dr. Standish will explain what has happened, and the conditions which must be expected in the near future.'

The president sat down and Dr. Standish rose. In essence his address covered in detail the facts he had given Morris Arnside. When he finished a murmur went over the gathering. Then Brice Torrington got up.

'Dr. Standish, the information you have given us is appalling to the last degree. In your opinion, how long have we before the sun becomes extinct?'

'At the most, two years. Maybe less.'

'And at the end of that period?'

'I foresee nothing but a frozen planet from which all life has been driven – probably underground. The seas and the air will freeze, to later escape into the vacuum of interstellar space. The light of the sun will be equal to that of a full moon, and its heat no greater.'

'And is there no scientific way in which the sun can be revived before it finally becomes a white dwarf?' the president asked anxiously.

'No way that we know of, Mr. President,' said Standish. 'I had hoped that there might have been present among us one person who could perhaps have helped us. I mean Miss Brant – or, as she is more probably called – the Golden Amazon. Her science alone might be of an order to restore the sun, but I have tried for many months to get in touch with her without success. Doesn't anybody know where she is?' he implored, spreading his hands. 'Mr. Wilson, she is partly a relative of yours, is she not? Have you no idea?'

Chris Wilson stood up to reply. 'She does not tell me or my family any more than she tells anybody else, doctor. I have not the least idea what has become of her this last 18 months.'

'As regards that,' Torrington said. 'I have something to say, if I am permitted the floor, Mr. President?'

'By all means, Mr. Torrington.'

'I believe,' Torrington said deliberately, 'that this superwoman – this scientific creature with the strength of 10 men and the scientific skill of a witch – has taken revenge upon us people of Earth and departed to places unknown, maybe to the other side of the Universe. From the very outset of her career, her avowed aim has been to control the world. Fifty-two years ago, in 1980, she was three years of age. A surgical genius experimented upon her during that time, altered her gland structure, and believed that she would grow up into a woman who could blot out war. Her altered gland structure gave her the strength of 10 powerful men together with a beauty never seen in a normal woman. And ageless life! Long has she boasted that she will live at least 500 years. When last seen 18 months ago she looked only 25.'

'This is purely a recital of known facts,' the president commented.

'Mr. President, I am refreshing the memory of those who forget this woman's real upbringing. She was adopted by the parents of Mr. Wilson's wife and grew up alongside the girl whom Mr. Wilson later married. When she became a woman the wonder girl's staggering scientific power made her attempt the conquest of London as a prelude to mastering the world. She was beaten in that. Then she apparently turned over a new leaf and gave us valuable scientific secrets. She showed us how to control atomic force. She mastered space. She gave us Venus and Mars and the Moon for colonies. She gave us untold wealth by the transmutation of elements. But that woman hates us! She has said so time and again. Therefore, what more natural than when she had the chance, she should try and destroy us all? That I believe she has done, and left us forever.'

'You mean that you think she is the cause of this solar disaster?' the president asked, puzzled.

'There's no doubt about it! Ask Dr. Standish. If she had not flung that Martian armada in the sun it would have been as normal as ever today. I insist that she did it knowing what the later effect would be. Unable to conquer us by her own methods she has used cosmic means to do it. Probably, even now, she is somewhere listening and laughing at our discomfiture.'

'That's a lie!' Ethel cried, leaping up with flaming cheeks beside her father. 'You've no right to accuse my Aunt Vi like that!'

'She is not your aunt, Miss Wilson,' Torrington corrected, with a cynical smile. 'However, I assume you call her such purely as a term of endearment.'

'Never mind what I call her! There isn't a word of truth in your statement – Stop tugging at me, dad!' Ethel broke off angrily. 'I'm going to have my say! Listen, all of you. I know Miss Brant better than any of you. I've been with her during her exploration of other worlds. She has saved my life many times, and all of yours, and not taken a scrap of credit. How dare you say she's trying to destroy us?'

The metal king said: 'Miss Brant is not a normal woman with feminine sentiments, but a scientific machine utterly pitiless in her methods. If she is not willing to let us die in the midst of this solar catastrophe, why doesn't she come forward in our hour of dire need?'

'There must be a good reason,' Ethel retorted.

'Yes, indeed!' Torrington agreed.

'Sit down, Rosy!' Chris urged.

'I'll not have Aunt Vi's name blackened in her absence. If she were here herself Mr. Torrington wouldn't dare say such things.'

'If she were here there'd be no need,' Torrington observed. He turned to face the president again.

'Mr. President, unless the Amazon returns and explains her conduct satisfactorily it is the opinion of myself and my colleagues that she should be put under technical arrest. That is, should she ever be found she must be brought to trial to explain why she has remained absent and deprived us of her skill. She is a servant of the public, and knows it.'

'You mean she should be brought to the bar of the Tribunal of Justice?' the president asked.

'I do. I am prepared to admit that in many ways, she has helped us in the past, but deep down she has always been a menace – and I remain unshaken in my belief that she only threw that Martian armada into the sun because she knew it would destroy the sun and us. She stands today in our eyes as the greatest scientific criminal in history.'

Torrington did not stop here. His speech obviously had been prepared in consultation with the higher-ups in world affairs, and so skilfully did he emphasize his points that at the finish there did not appear to be a single redeeming feature in the character of the mysteriously absent Amazon.

'Very well,' the president agreed. 'Should Miss Brant return she will be put under arrest and made to explain her actions in court. Now we must turn to the vital matter at issue. How do we save ourselves from this disaster?'

'We must go underground,' Dr. Standish answered. 'I am not an engineer, but I understand from Mr. Torrington and others that the problem of tunnelling below the earth and installing vast underground habitats filled with every modern necessity is not beyond possibility. If we do not do this we shall die in the frozen wastes which are inevitably coming. Travelling to other worlds in the system will not help us, either, since they rely on the same sun.'

Torrington got on his feet again. 'This, Mr. President, is surely a matter to be settled in a more personal atmosphere? I have around me the men who can build the shelters, arrange the food distribution, control the transport . . . It will mean that every living being must be indexed, and all available space must be mapped out—'

Chris Wilson and Ethel did not wait to hear any more. They went out silently from the hall, and Ethel asked: 'Do you scent a deliberate plot, dad?'

Chris nodded soberly. 'As far as the technical arrest of your Aunt Vi is concerned, yes – but it doesn't worry me unduly because if she ever does return she knows how to take care of herself and I'm pretty sure she'll have a reasonable explanation. What does worry me is that Torrington will be in charge of building the shelters. I don't trust him. I remember once when he had an order for four new space liners and each one of them had faulty metal. They'd have sent thousands of people to their deaths if your aunt hadn't discovered the flaws with testing equipment. Torrington had to put things right – and I think that incident with others, is lingering in his mind. That no doubt is one reason why he wants your aunt's arrest.'

CHAPTER V

In the weeks which followed the decision to honeycomb the earth, mass-hysteria swept the world. The suicide graph leapt to a fantastic height. At the other end of the scale were those who were determined to enjoy themselves in the two remaining years, no matter what the cost. Crime, mob violence, religious revival – they marched side by side.

Control, law, order – all vanished in two weeks. Never had the world been so much in need of a leader. Never had the human race appeared so much like an overturned anthill. Everybody was doing something, subconsciously aware that even when done it would probably be wasted effort. The more devout prayed.

Ethel attended many of the London services for deliverance from the approaching catastrophe. She prayed, too, for the safety of her beloved Aunt Vi, wherever she might be.

In three weeks there was a sudden exodus of private space machines, their owners determined to find other worlds, no matter how dangerous, where there was at least a sun. That they could never reach another world with a sun in the space of a human lifetime was something which never occurred to them.

Chris Wilson completed his plans for retirement to Brazil. He felt that he was justified. The Dodd Space Line had ceased to operate – at least with safety. The terrific electronic disturbances created by the gigantic sunspots made space unsafe to navigate. Instruments would not register and radio contact with Earth was impossible.

Further, there was danger in staying much longer in Britain. A giant glacier was creeping down from the Arctic Circle and might at any time accelerate its movement and bury the British Isles for ever under its unfathomable weight . . . Already the northern United States had become uninhabitable with a persistent 400 below zero temperature. People were moving by every possible means to the Brazilian areas, to the

Sahara, to India, the Persian Gulf, the Gold Coast – anywhere indeed where a semblance of warmth remained. Apart from these places and other favoured climes – as yet – there was a breath of icy doom in the air as the dark areas on the face of the sun grew visibly larger with each passing day.

Chris Wilson, with a few final matters to attend to, sent Ethel ahead of himself and his wife. Ethel had instructions to fly straight to Brazil by the 10 a.m. air liner, open up the residence, and stay until her mother and father joined her. But it was an instruction easier to give than carry out.

People constantly besieged the airports, attacking passengers who were flying to a temporary haven, and Ethel was no exception to the threat of violence. When she left her car at the airport to board the liner chartered by a number of prominent people, Ethel found herself followed by a menacing crowd of men and women who were at the entrance gates.

Then she saw that the crew and pasengers were being held in the midst of a second large group. She glanced behind her: there was no escape that way.

'What's the meaning of this?' she asked. 'What right have any of you to behave in this fashion?'

A man said: 'There've bin enough flights to better spots an' we're stoppin' it until we get a fair deal. The government should arrange for everybody to go – an' until they do nobody goes!'

'Take your hands off me,' Ethel yelled, as the man seized her by the arm. 'Get away from me—'

Instead two other men joined in and Ethel found herself moved along helplessly. She kicked, scratched, and writhed violently as her three particular captors bore her along.

Then there was an interruption. A big car came sweeping through the crowd and stopped a few feet from the struggling Ethel.

The three men holding her stared in wonder as another woman came into view, thrusting through the people – a tall girl, hatless, her vividly blonde hair flowing in the biting wind. The white costume she was wearing seemed utterly inadequate in the cold.

'Well, this one walks right into it,' one of the men commented, releasing Ethel. 'I'll deal with 'er and you stick to—'

The man never finished his sentence. He had a momentary glimpse of a slender, white-clad arm lashing out at him with the speed of a striking snake – then the universe seemed to him to explode in blinding light. The blow he received on the jaw flung him a good six feet away where he crashed on his face motionless.

'Aunt Vi!' Ethel screamed. 'Oh, thank heaven you've come!'

Abruptly she was free. In the pale light the other two men had just realized who the newcomer was. Now they saw tawny yellow skin, a wierdly beautiful face and dark pools of violet eyes.

'The Golden Amazon!' one of them gulped, and turned to run.

He was unlucky. With the speed of a tigress, the Amazon caught up with him and his companion. Her hands gripped each of them at the backs of their necks. A sudden tautening of her steel-strong fingers and a twist of her wrists – the men fell, and did not rise again.

Ethel came racing forward. 'Aunt Vi, whatever happened to you? Why were you away so long, and—'

'Never mind that now,' the Amazon interrupted, catching the girl's arm. 'Our first job is to get to safety. This mob looks ugly. If I can reach my car again we'll be okay.'

She swung round, still holding Ethel. The men and women had now gathered in a circle, intent on revenge for the ruthless manner in which several of their number had been mown down by the car. The queerly-shaped, shining vehicle, its doors immovably locked, was surrounded by the mob. Ethel hesitated but the Amazon forced her onwards, ready for whatever challenge might come. Within a few feet of the grim-faced rioters she paused and looked round on them.

'I warn you,' she said, 'that if you make the least attempt to block my progress or that of Miss Wilson and these other ladies and gentlemen who are to board this liner, you'll be extremely sorry.'

'You've some room to talk!' one of the men shouted. 'But for you things wouldn't be in the mess they are! We know all about it – how you ran out on us!'

The Amazon looked mystified for a moment and glanced inquiry at Ethel – but she had no time to ask questions. She looked towards the men and women who should have taken the air liner and who were still in the grip of the rioters.

'Fight for your liberty!' she shouted. 'If you can get free get aboard the liner. I'll take care of everything here.'

The onsurging crowd knew perfectly well what they were attempting as far as the Amazon was concerned, but they were convinced that weight of numbers would win. What they did not expect was the Amazon's last-second move. From her costume pocket she whipped a small object like a torch and pressed the button. Into the faces of the men and women rioters there flooded a purple-tinted mist. They stopped in their tracks, staggered, then sagged helplessly to the ground.

'Keep to windward of this vapour!' the Amazon said to Ethel, puffing it forth relentlessly. 'It produces two-hour paralysis. Quick, Ethel – to the car!' She shouted: 'You other people get into the liner!'

Angling her way so as to keep to the rear of the wind-floated gas the Amazon moved toward her car. Ethel by her side and the men and women belonging to the air liner heading toward it. Here and there, where she was not quick enough to use her gas gun, the Amazon used a fist – with poleaxing effect. So she gained the car and pressed a button and one door opened.

'In you get, Ethel.'

Ethel half fell in and the Amazon slid in beside her. The car hurtled forward, sweeping through those rioters who made a last desperate effort to attack, and on through the gateway.

The Amazon returned the gas gun to her pocket and gave a taut little smile.

'You left it a bit late to come back, aunt, didn't you?' Ethel asked, her eyes wide.

'Taking me to task, Rosy?' the Amazon asked, drily.

'Of course not! Only things are in a terrible mess and everybody seems to have gone crazy. It's because of the sun. It's dying.'

'Yes . . .' The Amazon looked through the transparent roof

of the car at the saffron ball glowing balefully overhead. 'So I believe.'

'Where have you been these past 18 months?' Ethel insisted. 'Didn't you know what was going on – how badly we all need your help?'

'What did that lout back there mean by my running out on you?' the Amazon asked.

'You don't know? Why, everybody thinks you caused this solar disaster and then left us to our fate. There's a warrant out for your arrest if you can be found.'

'We'll talk later,' the Amazon said. 'I want to get to your home before mother and father leave for Brazil. Then maybe we can have a talk.'

'But do you think it's safe? The airport crowd knows you've come back; they'll tip off the police and you'll be arrested.'

'I'll deal with that if I have to. There are other matters first.'

CHAPTER VI

Chris Wilson and his wife, both of them wrapped in furs, were waiting on the steps of their London residence when the Amazon's car reached it. She opened the door, jumped out, and Ethel followed her.

'So she was all right?' Chris asked in relief, putting an arm about Ethel's shoulders. 'Thank heaven for that—'

'You should have more sense, Chris, than let the girl try to take an airliner, as things are!' the Amazon snapped. 'The mob had got her when I reached the airport. You're lucky to have her back in one piece.'

'I knew it was wrong!' Chris Wilson found his wife giving him a grim look. 'We should have used a private plane—'

'They're not safe, dear! Besides, I'm not as good a pilot as I used to be.'

'Let's get inside,' the Amazon suggested. 'I've one or two matters to discuss.'

She led the way through the big hall and into the lounge and switched on the lights.

'Aren't you cold, Vi, in that summer costume?' Chris Wilson's wife asked in wonder, tugging off her furs.

'You know me better than that,' the Amazon smiled, seating herself. 'Sit down, all of you, and let's try and get matters straight.'

Chris, his wife and Ethel seated themselves and waited. For a moment or two the Amazon did not say anything. She seemed to be thinking, her slender amber-tinted fingers tapping pensively on the chair arm. Chris Wilson noticed that she was as beautiful as she had always been. Over 50, she was apparently as young as Ethel.

'I've been in space,' she said abruptly, evidently deciding at which point to start speaking.

'We guessed as much,' Chris responded. 'But what doing?'

'Trying to find a way to cure the sun.' The Amazon smiled

cynically. 'You don't suppose I have been in ignorance of what the sun has been doing, do you?'

'Well, no,' Chris admitted, 'but we did rather wonder—'

'Why I stayed away so long? I did it to get some peace. As long as I am on Earth here every little problem, scientific or ordinary, is dumped in my lap. I had much more important work to do and I didn't want to be interrupted. I was not aware, though, of the rumpus going on here because I received no radio reports. The static interference of the sun spots blocked all communications. It was when I noticed that Earth was looking in a sorry state through advancing icecaps that I decided to come back and see what was happening.

'Early this morning I arrived, as you know, Chris. I left my Ultra at home and motored here, after finding you were not at your office. You told me about Ethel and I realized from the mobs I'd seen that she might be in trouble, so I went after her.'

'So that was it,' Ethel exclaimed. 'And you lived in space in the Ultra for 18 months?'

'In the Ultra I could live in space indefinitely. It is fitted with every necessity.'

'Whereabouts in space were you?' Chris asked.

'Between the orbits of Mars and Jupiter. I have never been that far distant before. I did it so that the disturbances from the sun would not affect my instruments. Unfortunately my experiments didn't amount to anything. I failed to find what I was seeking.'

For some reason she did not amplify her statement but instead passed on to other matters.

'From what I can gather. I am supposed to be the cause of all the trouble going on at present. What exactly are the facts?'

Chris Wilson gave them to her, with outbursts from Ethel at intervals. There was a glint in the Amazon's purple eyes when the story had been told.

'So that is the situation,' she mused. 'In other words, a propaganda campaign by Brice Torrington, aimed against me – and from the look of things he has managed the job of inflaming the people quite successfully.'

'If you're caught you'll inevitably be brought before the Tribunal of Justice,' Chris said anxiously.

Ethel said, 'I'd like to know what chance the sun has got of being restored.'

The Amazon looked at her for a moment, then compressed her lips.

The Amazon said: 'Unless I can find what I'm looking for the sun will never be restored. I knew 18 months ago, when the first spots appeared, what was coming – and of course the reason; but in fairness to myself I must say that I didn't think of it at the time I flung that Martian armada in the sun. However, the thing is done now. I've worked night and day, using every scientific trick I know, to find just one thing. I call it atomium. It exists in the universe – crystallized energy, possessing a force so prodigiously powerful that beside it atomic power is nothing but a cheap firework.'

'I never heard of it.' Chris wrinkled his brow.

'Not by that name, since I christened it. But 60 years ago certain famous scientists declared that it did exist, at least in theory – and is only to be found in space. It is energy – the essence thereof, if you wish – compressed into a mineral-like structure by the forces which exist in space. It is formed in much the same way as steam vapour forms into water by the action of condensation. My instruments here on Earth, which I built specially for the job, showed me that the stuff existed in space, so I set out to find it. I became a sort of cosmic fisherwoman waiting to catch some of these drifting atomium meteors in my magnetic grapples – but I didn't even catch a glimpse of the stuff.'

'And yet your instruments showed they were there?' Ethel asked, surprised. 'That was queer, wasn't it?'

'The sun ruined my experiments,' the Amazon snapped. 'The discharges of energy he keeps sending through space upset all the instruments. They were incapable of recording the presence of atomium, or anything else. All they did was record the sun's disturbance . . . so I had to fish by blind chance and got nothing. What is needed is something to cut out the sun's interference, but if I do that I shall have to make my instruments insensitive, so . . .'

She sighed. 'For the moment I'm beaten. My only hope is to go back into space and hunt for atomium on the off chance that I'll find it. That may take years, and by then it will be too late. Once the sun has become a white dwarf nothing can restore him.'

'You mean,' Chris said, 'that if you could find some atomium you could restore the sun?'

'I know I could. Mathematically, I know what atomium can do; my task would be to make the theory practical. Atomic discharge will continue in the sun until he finally collapses . . . A vast boost in his internal energy, such as atomium could give, would start the atomic cycle going again and in building up new temperatures he could restore himself to his former level and the danger of collapse would disappear. It is all a matter of bringing him back to his critical temperature between 4·88 and 3·54.'

'But in the meantime,' Ethel said, 'you think it best for everybody to go below?'

'Nothing else can be done,' the Amazon responded. 'Go below by all means. I shall do likewise as the surface becomes unbearable. I only wish that Torrington were not the man behind the shelters.'

Ethel said: 'He isn't to be trusted. If only the law were not after you, Aunt Vi, you could examine the metal Torrington proposes to use and make sure it's the right stuff. I can't see him playing a straight game even if he does know it's the end of the world.'

She glanced out of a window and saw that two large cars had just come up to the front door.

'Apparently the news of my return has reached the police,' she commented. 'I have to go immediately. Carry out your plan, Chris, and go to Brazil. You'll have a bit of comfort for a few months at least. I'll join you there when I can.'

She opened the French windows and stepped outside, but her intention of a swift departure in her car was forestalled. Two armed policemen barred her path, their guns trained on her. She relaxed and shrugged as they came forward. True to her policy of never fighting when the odds were too heavily against her, she stood waiting.

'Evidently our chief of police remembers all avenues of

escape,' she commented, then she pivoted round as an inspector and two sergeants came hurrying into view.

The inspector said. 'Miss Brant – alias the Golden Amazon – you are under arrest. If you will come with us to headquarters the technical charges preferred against you will be stated. I have to warn you that—'

'You needn't,' the Amazon interrupted. 'I'll come without giving you any trouble. In fact I'm rather anxious to verify my suspicion as to the person or persons behind this farce. For it is a farce, inspector, as perhaps you realize?'

'My personal opinion has nothing to do with the case, Miss Brant. If you will come with us—?'

'Very well. What of my car?'

'One of my men will ride with you – and I would warn you against trying any tricks.'

The Amazon smiled. 'That's very thoughtful of you. Shall we be going?'

CHAPTER VII

The Amazon's return and her trial before the Tribunal of Justice had the effect for the time being of taking people's minds off the worry of the dying sun and shelter digging. Those who could possibly manage it attended the trial. The Wilson family was not represented. Following the Amazon's suggestion, they had gone to Brazil, satisfied that the Amazon herself was the only one capable of extricating herself from her predicament.

Completely calm, the Amazon stood in the dock on the appointed morning. Well to the front of the courtroom were Brice Torrington, Morris Arnside and Ralph Swainson of the Atomic Power Corp. She smiled. Her three most deadly enemies, those who had striven to rid themselves of her scientific surveillance.

The public prosecutor recited the details of the accusation, to which the Amazon listened with an expression which suggested her mind was miles away. It was. Then she was forced to give her attention to the prosecutor as he stood before her.

'You are Violet Ray Brant, otherwise known as the Golden Amazon?'

'I am,' the girl agreed.

'Have you anything to say in regard to the charges levelled against you?'

'Yes – but I don't expect you to believe me. You are all obviously determined to discredit me, no matter what I might say in my own defence. I knew what had happened to the sun long before the astronomers discovered it, and since that time I have been trying to find a remedy.'

'And have you?' the prosecutor asked, hope of salvation from the impending catastrophe making him forget his legal status for the moment.

'I have not – and if you condemn me I never shall. I'm looking for a metal at present theoretical, called atomium.'

There was a pause. The Amazon's statement had had just

the effect she intended – and she pressed home the advantage.

'Gentlemen, you don't just condemn me when you pass judgment; you condemn everybody on the Earth! You know me to be the greatest scientist alive today. I am not an egotist. I state a fact. I have it almost within my grasp to overcome the danger which threatens us – to even rekindle the dying sun, but to do it I must have freedom of action. If I am not given it you assign yourselves and the rest of humanity to the underworld forever!'

Brice Torrington jumped up. 'Words, words, words,' he shouted, shaking an angry finger at the Amazon. 'This woman has always been a smooth talker. She can get out of any tight corner by using subtlety.'

The prosecutor cleared his throat. 'Miss Brant, what proof have we that you have been searching for this – er – atomium?'

'None, since it only exists in theory; but you have got proof that I don't intend to run away. Otherwise I wouldn't have come back to Earth.'

'I suggest you came back to Earth because you realized that in the existing confusion you might assume leadership,' the prosecutor snapped. 'From that it would be a short step to ruling the world, as you have always wanted.'

The Amazon sighed. 'Have it as you will. I said you would all disbelieve me because that is your avowed intention . . . I would mention, though, that I am only in this court because it suits my purpose to be so. I could have escaped from the guards who arrested me; I could have broken the bars of my cell with my bare hands; I could even have hypnotized you, Mr. Prosecutor, into failing to build up a case against me.' Her strange eyes smouldered at him so that he felt obliged to look down at his notes to escape her gaze. 'But I have used none of my powers because I want legal permission to carry on with my work and overcome this solar catastrophe. I can only get it by the court finding me innocent.'

'You knew all this would happen when you threw that Martian armada in the sun?' Torrington shouted.

'Not at the time. If you were in danger of being drawn into the sun, Mr. Torrington, you wouldn't stop and weigh scientific possibilities. You would fight for survival, as I had to do.'

'Words,' the metals king breathed. 'All words. This woman is a public menace.'

'The court will recess while the jury considers its verdict,' the judge announced, and the Amazon turned away with two wardresses at either side of her.

Twenty minutes later she was recalled to the dock. The judge glanced at her, then turned to the jury.

'Gentlemen of the jury, have you considered your verdict?'

'We have, sir.'

'And how do you find the prisoner? Guilty or not guilty?'

'Guilty – on all counts.'

The Amazon's expression did not change. The judge turned to her again.

'Miss Brant, would it not have been better had you had a counsel for the defence instead of conducting your own?'

'No counsel could have put it better than I did.'

'Have you any further statement to make before judgment is passed upon you?'

'I have. You are all fools, throwing away your one chance of salvation because Brice Torrington orders it! Whatever you may decide to do to me, I shall come back and right this injustice in whatever way I see fit. And I shall remember you three – Torrington, Arnside and Swainson!'

'Normally,' the judge continued, 'the penalty for your crimes, Miss Brant, would be death in the lethal chamber, but, possessing as you do a supernatural constitution, it is doubtful if the gas would have effect. So I am prescribing another penalty, as I am empowered to do under law. It is banishment. You will be sent from Earth in a—'

'Coffin ship?' the Amazon interrupted. 'I rather expected it. Torrington and his satellites would never rest while I remained on Earth, alive or dead. You will fire me out into space to that spot where great criminals have been sent – the dividing line between Earth and Moon. There, chained in my coffin ship, I will circle the Earth forever, the ship held by exactly balanced gravity of Earth and Moon gravity fields.'

'That,' the judge agreed, 'is the punishment. And it will be carried out tonight at sunset.'

The Amazon said no more. She turned away with her jailers and disappeared from the dock.

That same evening, at what would normally have been sunset, the Amazon was marched from her cell in the midst of armed guards and out into the quadrangle of the great jail.

She submitted to being thrust inside the narrow, tubular rocket which would carry her into outer space. Once inside it a thin band of case-hardened steel snapped into place about her waist, automatically locking itself. Another pinned her ankles close together, then two triple-linked chains were attached to wrist cuffs and snapped into their sockets.

The judge, a dim figure amidst the lights and whirling snow, uttered a few ceremonial words prescribed by law and then the airlock was locked on the outside. Then the Amazon set her teeth as with a sudden acceleration the rocket was fired. It tore through the tumult of the night – upward, onward, through atmosphere and troposphere, and onwards into the eternal silence of space. The glimmer of the sun shone drab gold through the two tiny portholes.

Its initial take-off speed somewhat lessened, there being just enough velocity to keep the rocket going against the pull of Earth's gravity, the Amazon found the pressure more bearable. She began to breathe with greater freedom.

She looked through the nearest port. Earth was below, a giant half planet, one side cloaked in night; the other wan and white-patched where the deadly glaciers were advancing.

The sun, though plainly dying, was still alive enough to give light, dimly yellow though it was. Here, with no air intervening, the mighty chasms gouged in his once unbearably brilliant face were depressingly obvious.

Her survey completed the Amazon peered through the opposite porthole. The Moon was there, at the full, only faintly discernable because of the diminished light coming from the sun. When the hurtling coffin ship reached the balance line between Earth and Moon gravity-fields the rocket would cease its onward motion. Instead it would then follow an elliptical orbit, balanced exactly between the two fields so that it would forever circle the Earth as long as gravity remained.

For a while the Amazon relaxed, then she pulled on the

chains holding her wrists to the metal walls of the rocket. No extra precautions had been taken. The coffin ship was of the conventional pattern used for criminals, but none of them had possessed the strength of the Golden Amazon.

By bringing her hands together the length of chain permitted her to cross her wrists, gripping the right chain with her left hand, and the left with the right. Then she began to pull, throwing every vestige of her power into the effort. At first she was unsuccessful, so she took a firmer grip, relaxed for several moments – then again threw her stupendous muscular strength into the struggle. Gradually the links began to bend. She twisted and turned them until they scorched her flesh, but each time they bent they became weaker until at last one of them snapped. With one hand free it only took the Amazon 30 seconds to finish the remaining links and her arms were free, the cuffs still clamped on her wrists with lengths of chain dangling from them.

The steel hoop about her waist was a tougher proposition. It refused to yield to direct treatment so she leaned her left arm over it, drawing her forearm beneath it and gripping the hoop half way down. By this method she could use her arm as a lever. She began forcing her arm backwards, her fingers gripped like pliers around the steel. It bent slightly but did not give way. Instead it tore loose from its locking clamp and waggled free.

The same treatment made short work of the ankle hoops and she rolled off the hard, narrow bed on to the floor where she lay thinking out what to do next. There was no opportunity to stand up. The rocket ship was only made to carry a recumbent passenger.

Without troubling to look, she knew that the rocket had no controls of any kind. It was mathematically timed to fall into the demarcation line and there stop, so to find a means of halting it and return to Earth was impossible. To be free of the chains and hoops was one thing, but to turn the freedom to account was another.

'When I reach the deadline,' she muttered, 'I shall follow an elliptical orbit around the Earth. Yet one little push either way would send me crashing to either Earth or moon . . .'

She thought back to a time when she had once turned a machine around in space by pushing it from the outside – but here there was no way out of the vessel, and if there had been, she had no space suit she could wear.

Meditation seemed to be the only answer. She gave herself up to it, turning over every detail of the situation in her mind as the rocket hurtled through emptiness. To every problem she believed there was a scientific answer – but the rocket reached the end of its journey without her finding one.

She only became aware of the change in motion by degrees. Wriggling to the porthole, she saw that the moon was to one side and the Earth to the other. The Earth did not appear to move, which satisfied her that she was travelling in a circle around it.

CHAPTER VIII

She flogged herself into thinking furiously, lying on the narrow bed to which she had formerly been secured. As she meditated she gazed out on the depthless mysteries of space – then after a while it occurred to her that an object she had at first taken to be a star was coming nearer. Out in the void distances were deceptive. A star light-centuries distant might look pretty much the same as a smaller mass only a few thousand miles away.

It began to dawn on her that the mass was in fact an irregular but enormous chunk of cosmic rock, its chipped facets catching the anaemic glimmering of the sun. She watched it, fascinated – then in growing alarm. There was no longer any doubt but what it was coming straight in her direction, perhaps drawn by the slight gravitational mass the space rocket possessed.

'Atomium,' she whispered, her eyes wide. 'I could swear to it! Crystalline in formation, grey in colour. Normal space rock is black—'

She stopped, her mind reeling, before the contemplation of how much energy was in that enormous mass. From her own mathematical computations she knew that a square inch of the stuff was capable of destroying half a planet into vapour. Then this mass, if it really were atomium, could—

The conviction of sudden and explosive death was upon her. She remained rigid, watching, her hands clamped on the porthole ledge. The cosmic mass seemed suddenly to leap forward. It blotted out all the stars. It was visible for a moment with its pitted surface and shining facets, like a blood-red ruby in the sinister crimson-yellow glow of the sun – then the travelling rocket received a blow which keeled it wildly through space, flinging the Amazon from the bed and upon her face on the floor. She had time to wonder that the stuff had not blown her into eternity and the rocket as well, then she realized that the rocket ship was in the midst of a headlong fall.

Dizzy with the ghastly sensation of an endless drop, she got on to her knees, as high as she could, with her head touching the roof. Peering through the porthole, she saw that the mineral substance was gone. It had evidently struck the rocket ship a glancing blow, and careered off into space over the dividing line, destroying the hair-breadth balance, so that the vessel was now immovably chained to the Earth's gravity field and hurtling downward toward the planet with ever-increasing speed.

The Amazon relaxed again on the floor, on her back – the only position she could take up to gain a certain amount of relief from the bottomless falling. Roughly she calculated how long a drop was ahead of her – but before it could be completed, the atmospheric friction would turn the rocket into a meteorite and she would be sealed inside a coffin of blazing molton metal.

Only one possibility could save her from this fate. The walls of the machine might be thick enough to resist the heat before it landed. And when it did land? The rocket would dive deep down into the earth, the shock of the impact bringing instant death to the occupant.

Whichever way, the Amazon viewed the problem she could foresee nothing but her own extinction. Not that she feared death. Her chief concern was that so much was left undone. Convinced as she was that she had happened upon atomium at the very moment when she could not use it, she wanted nothing more in life in order to make yet another effort to locate and harness the stuff.

'Or maybe it wasn't atomium,' she whispered to herself. 'It didn't explode – so perhaps it was only rock after all. Unless maybe atomium doesn't explode by concussion.'

She gave up the effort of trying to solve the problem. The tremendous fall she was taking had made her sleepy. She could not tell whether hours or minutes had passed before she was suddenly jerked into alertness again by a rising scream from outside the machine.

Atmosphere! And the rocket ship was slicing through it at thousands of miles an hour. Immediately grey clouds blanked down on the portholes, lighted presently by a fiery glow as the outer plates fused and sizzled under the stupendous friction.

Down and down, faster and faster, with a terrible din

deafening her ears. The Amazon shut her eyes and clenched her fists, tensed for the terrific impact of striking Earth. The heat became insufferable, and the spent air scorchingly hot.

Then the crash came. It hurled her two feet up from the floor and back again, a crumbled heap in a corner of the little cabin. The vessel still seemed to go down and then up again, amid the din of exploding jets of steam and rupturing hot plates.

Rocking gently to and fro, the rocket ship stopped its wild plunging. Stunned, the Amazon lay motionless, entirely unaware that the walls had split by the abrupt plunging of the white-hot vessel into the Pacific ocean. Now the water was commencing to trickle through, collecting in a pool on the floor, rising steadily, giving the rocket a keel which prevented it rocking. Utterly knocked out, the Amazon lay where she was.

But outside the rocket things were happening. From grey vapours and storm clouds a queerly designed, wingless machine glided down silently, and came to rest on the water. Here in these once sub-tropic regions the temperature had not yet reached freezing point. The odd machine moved rapidly until it was touching the sides of the fallen rocket. A man appeared through an opened airlock. He was tall, massively built, covered from head to foot in a curious one-piece garment which had the gleam of gold. Even his hair and ears were imprisoned in a rubber-like cowl.

With a lithe movement he leaped to the rocket and seized the edge of the topmost riven plates. With the strength of a Hercules he bent them gradually away from each other and then jumped down into the narrow darkness. In the space of a few moments he had swept up the unconscious Amazon in his arms and carried her to his own vessel. He closed the airlock and then sat down beside a complicated control board, watching as the Amazon slowly recovered on the wall bed on which he had lain her.

He smiled to himself as he noticed the strength and slenderness of her figure, the yellowness of her skin, the almost breathtaking beauty of her features even in unconsciousness. Turning, he picked up an instrument like a hypodermic needle and bent over the girl, plunging it into her arm. She stirred, gasped a little, and then opened her eyes.

She could not believe what she saw. The features of her rescuer were strong, apparently young, and most certainly handsome. He loosened the cap from his ears and head as she stared at him, and there was released a shock of vividly blond hair, as golden as her own. Eyes, a curious shade of reddish blue, considered her in kindly good nature.

'Better?' he inquired, putting a powerful arm behind her shoulders and raising her slightly.

'Much better, thank you.' The Amazon jerked free of his grip with an indignant glance. 'What – what happened? Where are you from?'

The stranger stood up and the Amazon's wide violet eyes followed his stature from head to toe. He was possibly six feet, eight or ten inches tall, and muscled like a Greek god. The strength of his frame was visible even through the close-fitting gold-hued tunic he was wearing.

'I am afraid,' he said, in the quietest of voices, 'that you would have died had I not rescued you from that rocket. It had burst and water was pouring into it. So I brought you here.'

The Amazon glanced about the unfamiliar control room, and the equally, unfamiliar control board. She had never seen a machine quite like this in all her experience. Then she noticed the hermetically sealed windows and the big rubber sheath over the airlock.

'This is a space ship,' she ejaculated suddenly.

'Yes, indeed,' the young giant agreed gravely.

'Then . . .' Frowning, the Amazon set her feet on the floor and scooped the disordered hair from her face. 'Who are you?' she insisted.

'My name is . . .' He seemed to hesitate. 'Abna,' he said.

'Oh?'

Abna smiled and white teeth gleamed. 'You are limiting your range, Miss Brant,' he told her. 'Recently you travelled much farther than Mars or Venus. You went nearly as far as Saturn, operating between his orbit and Jupiter on one occasion, while on another you spent a lot of time between Jupiter and Mars in the region of the asteroids.'

'I cannot see,' the Amazon said, 'what that has to do with it.'

'I am Abna of Jupiter,' the giant explained. 'Or at least that is what you call my world. We know it as Vaz, but that is beside the point.'

The Amazon's violet eyes narrowed at him. 'I don't believe you,' she said bluntly, standing up. 'Jupiter has a high ammonia content in his atmosphere. Such a man as you, essentially Earthly – even if you are on the big side – could never have evolved on a planet like Jupiter, with his huge gravitation. I would be more inclined to expect someone reptilian.'

'Perhaps,' Abna said, 'my appearance is occasioned by the fact that though I was born and raised on Jupiter, my ancestry belongs to Earth.'

'Impossible!'

'Not at all. You must have heard of Atlantis. Like every body else you must have wondered what became of the survivors of the continent of Mu?'

CHAPTER IX

The Amazon did not look up. In fact she was somehow feeling the indignity of being so much smaller than the man who had saved her. The top of her head barely reached his massive shoulders. Besides, his smile was irritating to her.

'Atlantis vanished at the time of the Deluge,' she said. 'Or so say our records. And the Azores represent the spot where Atlantis and the continent of Mu once stood, the Azores being the actual mountain tops of the sunken continent.'

'Exactly so,' Abna agreed. 'Please sit down, Miss Brant. You must be shaken after that fall you took.'

'I am perfectly all right, thank you.'

For answer he took her shoulders in his big hands, much as a strong man might hold a child. She attempted to pull loose but to her amazement was unsuccessful. The grip failed to dislodge and she was thrust gently but firmly into a sitting position on the wall bed. Then, as she gazed in wonder, Abna took a tool from the bench under the control panel and clipped through the manacles still on the Amazon's wrists, finally casting the metallic clamps aside.

'Now,' he said, taking a fixed chair near her. 'Let me explain.'

The Amazon just looked at him. For the first time in her life she had come across a man who was unaffected by her vast physical strength.

'There is ample evidence,' Abna said, 'to show that the people of Atlantis were brilliant scientists; your own scientists admit that. They were. They knew the Deluge was coming and made preparations to avoid it. Knowing that in future ages the inner circle of planets would be invaded by Earth colonists they chose a more distant world – namely Jupiter. On that planet there is one area which we converted to our own use – one solid continent 800 miles across, surrounded by the ammonia vapours and terrific storms which are Jupiter's normal lot. But on that one continent we thrive in an atmosphere rather like

Earth's and artificial means keep the gravitation suited to our constitutions.'

'We have a scientific race thousands of years ahead of anything Earth can produce, chiefly because we started so much sooner. So you see I am really a man of Earth. Nor is there much difference in our ages. I am, by Earth standards, nearly 60. You are 55, but have the secret of almost eternal life, thanks to the experiments of a scientist when you were only three years of age. We too have means to prolong life indefinitely.'

'You seem to know quite a lot about me,' the Amazon commented.

'I know all about you,' Abna stated. 'I have made it my business. Incidentally, my father is the chief scientist of our race, which ranks next in position to the actual ruler of the surviving Altanteans. In all there are about 3,000 of us.'

'And where on Jupiter is this continent you speak of?'

'Your astronomers call it the Great Red Spot, the only solid area in a molten world. Naturally, so that we shall not be visited by unwanted people we take care to render our continent apparently empty. It is a simple matter. Polarizing radiations which blank out light-waves and make the continent appear lifeless. Actually, there are cities, an artificial sun, progress, peace – everything.'

The Amazon relaxed slightly, impressed.

'Ever since the outset of your career on Earth we have followed your activities with interest,' he resumed. 'Chiefly by means of our radio-television instruments which enabled us to both watch and hear events on Earth, as well as learn the language. I was fascinated by your scientific skill and proud isolation. You represented to me everything that a woman should be – but our instruments were not powerful enough to reveal you in detail. That chance came when you worked for so long near our planet. Every day I studied you by x-ray telescope. I wanted to speak to you, to say how much I admired you – so finally I decided that I would. At that moment you departed for your own world. I trailed you by instruments, but you had a long start on me and I did not catch up until recently when, imprisoned in that rocket, you plunged into the ocean.'

'Yes, simple when explained,' the Amazon admitted. 'Since

you have studied my activities for so long you must know my ambitions, the things I have done—'

'We are all agreed back home that you are the greatest scientist the Earth has recently produced.' Abna said seriously. 'And certainly the most beautiful one. Though of course your science is still far behind ours.'

'I see.' The Amazon smiled cynically. 'I assume then that you are also aware that I am trying to find a way of curing the dying sun?'

'We conjectured that that was the purpose of your special experiments. We had no definite information, though, since our contact with Earth was lost when the sun spots produced interference.'

'You say you have an artificial sun lighting your world?' the Amazon asked after a moment or two.

'Yes,' Abna smiled a little. 'I know what you are thinking, Miss Brant – that we might be able to hand on to you the secret of our synthetic sun so that you can save this dying one of yours. Unfortunately the information would avail you nothing. Our sun – since we on Jupiter are at such a tremendous distance from the natural one – merely gives light, not heat. Jupiter has enough internal warmth of his own to keep us comfortable. A synthetic sun for light alone is simply created, especially when it has only to serve an area some 800 miles in radius. Your problem is much vaster – to rekindle a dying star so it can again bring life back to the freezing inner planets.'

'Given time,' the Amazon said, brooding. 'I will solve it. I have the means, almost within my grasp.'

The giant was silent for a while, considering her. Then he said: 'If there is anything I can do – or my knowledge of our advanced science can do – you have but to say so.'

A puzzled look came into the Amazon's eyes. She searched Abna's handsome face quickly.

'Abna, tell me something. Do you really mean that you crossed space to this freezing world just to meet me?'

'Certainly. I would have crossed the universe if necessary. My race has many beautiful women, many clever ones, but throughout my life I have looked for one particular type of woman – and I have found her.'

'Clearly,' the Amazon said quietly, 'you don't know all about me, Abna, otherwise you would realize that you are wasting your time.'

'Are you convinced that I am?'

The Amazon did not answer. For once she could not think of the right words. There was a simple directness about the man which threw her off balance. He was utterly unlike any man with whom she had dealt before. Finally she said:

'From a purely scientific viewpoint, Abna, we might make something of a partnership, since that is what you desire. You will at least learn that I am not the kind of woman to be swayed by anybody else. I'm a law unto myself I—'

She paused as she found him smiling at her.

'Don't you believe it?' she demanded.

'Why shouldn't I?'

She continued: 'I am looking for a mineral substance, crystallized energy, which I call atomium. After searching in vain for it in space, I believe it was the very substance which hit my coffin ship and hurled it to Earth. When I reach my laboratory and instruments I intend to search for its location again and, if need be, go in search of it in space. If I can only get enough of it I can find a way to use it to rekindle the atomic power of the sun. Just one thing makes me wonder if the stuff was atomium. It didn't explode when it struck my coffin ship.'

'It hardly would,' Abna said. 'This crystallized energy exists. We have known that for years, but impact does not detonate it. It demands supersonic vibration in the order of 3,000,000 vibrations a second. A frequency that high does not exist in outer space, and indeed supersonics cannot exist in a vacuum at all, only in atmosphere. So, to detonate the substance, you need supersonics and atmosphere.'

The Amazon's eyes glowed. 'At last I can talk to somebody who understands me!' she exclaimed. 'Somebody who can argue a scientific theory.'

'Somebody who, in some respects, knows far more about science than you do,' Abna added, still smiling.

The Amazon got to her feet in proud disdain and Abna rose too – massive yet respectful of her sex.

'You're proud of your knowledge, aren't you?' she asked curtly. 'Proud of knowing more about atomium than I do?'

'I am only proud of the fact that my knowledge can help you, Miss Brant.'

She turned away for a moment and considered; then she appeared to come to a decision.

'What I said about us being partners, Abna, stands. But first I have one or two personal issues to settle. Three men tried to murder me in that rocket ship and I think they should be taken care of. Not only are they a menace to me but to everybody. They're supposedly world leaders, but interested only in making fortunes. It is even possible that they have built faulty shelters.'

'Such traitors exist in any community. I agree with you that they should be eliminated. Name those you mean and I can take care of them for you.'

'I prefer to do it myself, thank you. Right now I must get to Brazil. I have my laboratory there – my relatives, too. From that point onward we'll decide what to do.'

Abna nodded and turned to the control board.

CHAPTER X

The westernmost shores of South America were fringed with ice when Abna flew his strange and immensely speedy craft above them, and indeed throughout the journey from mid-Pacific there had been evidence of icebergs and, here and there, pack-ice. The deadly cold was reaching its tentacles down gradually to the tropical regions.

The Amazon gave directions and finally Abna began to bring the machine down on the fringe of a forest.

'There, to the east,' the Amazon said, pointing through the bowed outlook window. 'You see that white dwelling with the grounds round it, that is our destination. I built it myself originally as a place to which I could retire when I wanted to experiment in peace . . . then I sold it to the husband of my foster-sister – a Mr. Wilson.'

'Head of the Earth terminal of the Dodd Space Line,' Abna murmured, nodding. 'Yes, I know.'

He touched the controls and the machine descended swiftly, finally alighting in the grounds of the white-fronted house. It had a deserted look.

'My relatives said they were coming here,' the Amazon said, frowning. 'Unless something changed their plans—'

Abna opened the airlock and stepped outside, helping the Amazon after him. Accustomed as she was to handling every situation for herself it came as quite a surprise to her to find she was accorded such chivalry. She even felt it necessary to comment – but before she could do so a lone figure came out of the home and hurried across the grounds.

'Chris!' the Amazon exclaimed; and as the giant glanced at her she added, 'My foster-sister's husband.'

'Vi!' Chris came up at a run, his hand extended. 'You're here – alive and safe – after the things the council did to you. We heard all about it, that you were fired into space. and . . . There was nothing we could do and the news stunned us.' Chris stopped, considering the giant who towered over him smiling in his usual friendly fashion.

'This is Abna,' the Amazon introduced. 'He saved my life when the rocket fell.' She sketched in the details.

'Atlantis?' Chris repeated vaguely, staring. Then he gave a shrug. 'Well, I suppose it's possible. With space travel an everyday fact why should we doubt Atlantis? New surprises are always turning up.'

'Are you alone here, Chris?' the Amazon asked, glancing toward the house. 'What of Ethel and—'

'She and her mother have gone back to London.' Chris shook his head rather moodily. 'I'm intending to follow them by the next air liner passing this route. There wasn't room on the one they took. It's no use staying here, Vi. Food's running out; the tropics are so overcrowded with people they can't be catered for. To my mind, it's better to go to the big underground shelter section that has just been opened in London – the first of a series. From all accounts there are glaciers on the way and once they cover the British shelters there'll be no escape from the underworld. I want to be down there with my wife and Rosy when that happens.'

'Yes, that's understandable,' the Amazon admitted. 'What about the scientific equipment I had under the house there?'

'I . . .' Christ hesitated. 'I destroyed it, Vi.'

'Destroyed it? Great heavens, what for?'

'When the radio said you had been fired into space I couldn't see any chance of you coming back, so rather than let your valuable instruments and secrets fall into the wrong hands, I decided to destroy everything.'

The Amazon smiled. 'And very wise, too. Sorry, Chris. That was all you could do. I still have my London laboratory, anyway, and that's where I'm going.'

'But you can't take the risk, Vi, with the danger from the glaciers. When they reach Britain, as they soon will, you'll—'

'There are ways of keeping a lab like mine clear of a glacier,' the Amazon said. 'You agree, Abna?'

He nodded. 'We can equip the laboratory with an energy shield which will counteract the cold. There is work to be done – to trace this atomium.'

The Amazon said: 'Get your luggage, Chris. Abna will fly both of us to London.'

Chris nodded and hurried back to the house. He reappeared, a suitcase in his hand, and climbed into the flyer's control room. The Amazon and Abna followed him in, and the journey began.

'Is this thing driven by atomic power?' Chris questioned, when at 10,000 feet they began a soundless onrush.

Abna smiled and half turned in the control chair. ' I don't wish to sound egotistical, Mr. Wilson, but to us of Jupiter, atomic force is what gunpowder is to you of Earth – ancient! This ship flies as it does by cutting out gravitation below and behind and using the mass attraction of objects ahead, such as mountains, oceans, and so forth.'

'To me, just a dream,' the Amazon whispered, gazing at him. 'I have always known, Abna, that that is true power. Bending natural forces to your own use, make them do the work – but I never mastered the scientific principles.'

'I will show you some day, in less strained circumstances,' he promised.

Conscious that he was in the presence of scientific genius Chris held his peace; then he became attentive as with a flick of a button Abna switched on the radio. An announcer's voice, speaking in English, came through.

'The latest bolometer reading of the sun, taken from Everest, shows the temperature of the sun to still be falling, ranging at present in the order of 10,000 centrigrade. Canada, northern Europe and Asia are now almost empty of people. Pack-ice is jamming the North Sea. The Great Glacier, which has its birth in the North Polar regions, is spreading irregularly and has now completely enveloped Greenland and Iceland and part of northern Canada. It is extending eastward toward Sweden, the British Isles and west Europe. From the south another glacier is approaching to meet it. The southernmost tips of Australia and Africa are no more than a day's distance from it at its present rate of progress.'

'Cheerful, isn't it?' Chris muttered, glancing up as the announcer paused for a moment.

Neither the Amazon not Abna spoke. Their faces were grim and thoughtful.

'Three more shelters have been opened in the London area,' the announcer resumed, 'one of them containing radio headquarters from which these bulletins will henceforth be broadcast. Interviewed today in his headquarters shelter, Brice Torrington, the metals tycoon and supply magnate for the shelters, said they can withstand the Great Glacier when it comes. The underworld is insulated and sheathed, and the metal walls are composed of iron, aluminium, beryllium, titanium, tungsten, silver and lead, in varying layers. All ventilation arrangements have been made and there seems to be no doubt—'

The Amazon reached out and switched off the radio.

'I owe Torrington a good deal,' she said slowly, 'and also Morris Arnside and Ralph Swainson, his two colleagues, for what they tried to do to me, but perhaps it had better wait. If Torrington is making a good job of the shelters there would be no sense in wiping him out. Besides, I am too desperately pushed for time in solving my own problems. Personal scores can be cleared up later.'

'You know these men better than I do, Miss Brant,' Abna commented. 'It is for you to say.'

'Do you think anything could be gained by some of the people – say the cream of the populace – going to your planet?' Chris asked. 'You seem to have a pleasant land on this –er – Great Red Spot of Jupiter.'

'True,' Abna agreed, 'but as things are, with so many people here already domiciled below, I doubt if anything could be done. It would need thousands of space machines, tremendous organization—'

'It is better,' the Amazon interrupted, 'to conquer our own difficulties. Abna, I've set myself to rekindle the dying sun, and I'll do it. Here and there maybe you will be able to help.'

'Gladly,' Abna agreed, with that half tolerant smile.

'Further,' the Amazon hurried on, 'it is better nobody sees me in the underworld; it might only inflame the people needlessly, thinking as they do about me after Torrington's propaganda against me. When they see results – such as a rekindled sun – then they will have to believe, and that will be the time to take care of Torrington for the injustice he has inflicted upon me.'

As the dim grey outlines of Britain began to appear, Chris turned towards his suitcase.

'I brought furs with me,' he said. 'I've an idea I'm going to need them.' He peered outside on the vessel. The outer plates were white with frost but the window was clear by reason of the defreezing equipment.

'There are furs for us in the locker, Miss Brant,' Abna said, glancing around from the control board. 'I came prepared for any eventuality from tropic to arctic. You'd better get ready.'

The Amazon turned to the storage compartment and put on one of the fur suits, with its big comfortable hood, face shield, and automatically heated gloves. Abna slipped in the automatic pilot for a moment or two while he too prepared; then masked like Arctic explorers, they stood looking through the window as, under the Amazon's directions, Abna began to lower the vessel.

'The main shelter I'm seeking is near Charing Cross,' Chris said. 'If you'll put me down there I'll find my way.'

'Best method,' the Amazon agreed. 'We'll be on our way again before anybody has the chance to ask questions.'

The machine dropped swiftly, buffeted by wind screaming out of the north. The sun had set and the cold, biting darkness of the Arctic night had descended. Using powerful floodlights, Abna guided his machine with unerring skill, sweeping low over rooftops and finally down into the very heart of London. He could do so in safety. There was no traffic worth mentioning. No street lights were functioning.

'Look after yourselves,' Chris said, as the airlock was opened and a frigid blast made him gasp for a moment. 'We'll be counting on you.'

' 'By, Chris . . .' Vi's gloved hand grasped his for a moment, and Abna did likewise – then Chris was gone into the darkness, his suitcases clenched in his fingers.

CHAPTER XI

Swiftly Abna shut the airlock and swept the vessel up into the air again to rooftop level.

'Where now?' he questioned.

'Only a mile or two; my home is on the city outskirts.'

Abna nodded and asked no more questions, concentrating on following out the Amazon's directions as she peered into the dark through the windows. So, without passing a single aircraft, her out-town residence was reached. Gently Abna brought the machine down outside a massive annexe to the house.

'It's the hangar for my spaceship, the Ultra,' the Amazon explained, moving the sheath from the door. 'If you will wait a moment I'll go inside and open the roof for you, then you can bring your vessel inside to safety. There'll be room enough for it.'

Abna nodded and the Amazon stepped outside. Quickly she hurried around the annexe to the front door of her home, opened the combination lock, and stepped inside. There was a dark silence greeting her. Her maid and confidant, Tana, was missing. Evidently she had joined the shelter refugees, convinced that her mistress was never returning.

Switching on the cold-lights as she went, the Amazon hurried through the house, the laboratory, and then to the hangar. A switch set the roof opening into two segments and presently Abna's strange craft came into view and came down gently in the flare of the floodlamps. The Amazon closed the roof after him and he stepped from the machine, loosening his furs as he did so. He gave the shining ovoid of the Ultra an interested study as he passed it.

'Lovely design,' he commented, 'but a trifle antique.'

'It suits my purpose,' the Amazon answered, nettled. 'If you'll come into the house I'll fix a meal for us.'

He followed her through the laboratory, where again he had a strangely amused expression as he glanced about him on the complicated instruments – and so into the big lounge. The Amazon switched on the atoheaters, drew the window shades, and then took off her furs.

'You'll find all the necessities for freshening up on the first floor, third door,' she said. 'I'll be back shortly.'

Instead of freshening up the young giant followed her across the hall and into the kitchen regions. This was a territory which in the ordinary way she never invaded, but Tana's absence now made it imperative. In silence Abna watched as the Amazon gathered together food in tabloid form and some bottles of restorative.

'I'll carry the tray,' he volunteered, as she added plates, glasses, and small silver tongs.

The Amazon shrugged: 'Very well.'

They went into the lounge once more and sat with the meal on a low table. Abna said:

'I suppose we're at fault. You and I, alone in this house of yours. From the technical point, however, as partners, there is nothing else we can do.'

'Nothing,' the Amazon agreed, 'and while we are on the subject, let me affirm my earlier statement – that we are strictly scientific partners, working together to restore a dying sun. There is nothing more to our association than that.'

'Of course not.' He smiled upon her pleasantly. 'Why should you assume there is?'

'I'm not. I'm just reminding you.'

'Oh.' Abna drank the restorative, his reddish-blue eyes fixed on the girl. They seemed to be laughing while his handsome face remained serious.

When they had finished their refreshment the Amazon led the way to the laboratory and motioned to the instruments.

'Everything here is at your disposal,' she said.

Abna went to the queerly fashioned occiligraph. Switching it on, he watched the wild, wavy lines blurring up and down the screen.

'Electronic energy from the sun spots,' the Amazon explained. 'They penetrate the Earth, of course, which is why the apparatus functions even though the sun is below the horizon.'

'I see . . .' Abna glanced around him. 'And which is your detector for atomium?'

The Amazon moved to a massive switch panel, lined with dials. She switched on the power from the atomic generators and the apparatus began to operate. The girl pointed to a needle flawlessly balanced inside a sealed vacuum globe.

'That's the detector itself,' she said. 'That needle, if there were not so much solar interference, would swing instantly to wherever the nearest atomium may be lying, principally because it is made to be sensitive to any great mass of energy – and atomium is more or less pure energy condensed into a solid. Before the sun spots became so severe the needle worked perfectly. You see it now – lifeless.'

Abna nodded but he did not say anything. He turned to the workbench with its litter of tools and equipment, and began to fashion an instrument. The Amazon watched him, a frown gathering.

'Is it a secret – or can you tell me what you're doing?' she asked.

'Hardly a secret. A better term would be "incomprehensible" – to you, that is.'

'You haven't a particularly high opinion of my scientific prowess, have you?' she asked drily.

'I have, but I know your limitations. You do not, for instance, know the precise wave-length of negative force necessary to counteract the sun's interference.'

'I never heard of negative energy,' the Amazon responded, 'and for another thing – if you know so much about it, why didn't you use it on Jupiter when you found the sun interfering with your contact with Earth?'

'I tried to, but my father would not listen. He said I only wanted non-interference so that I could study you, and therefore he considered the idea was needless.'

'I'm flattered,' the Amazon murmured.

He went on working industriously. There came once more to the Amazon the curious feeling of being dominated, but on this occasion it caused her less resentment. Abna had a way of being master of a situation without making her feel small. Deep down she realized she was undergoing emotional transitions such as she had never known before in her intensely individual, scientific life.

Rather than disturb Abna's concentration, she sat down and remained silent, watching.

It was close on midnight when he had finished. He relaxed and considered his work – rather like a highly complicated radio receiver – then he smiled at the Amazon.

'There it is,' he said. 'Fortunately you had all the necessities here. Now, let us see.'

Picking the instrument up he went over to the atomium detector and wired it and his own apparatus together.

'Switch on the power,' he said, and the Amazon closed the knife-switch. Then she stared – first at the occiligraph from which all trace of solar interference had gone, leaving a blank screen – and then at the detector needle which was pointing diagonally downward.

'It works!' she ejaculated.

'Naturally,' Abna said. 'Your detector is now shielded by a core of negative energy which repels outside interference. To explain more than that would involve physics of such a high order that even you would not understand – with all due respect to your genius, Miss Brant.'

The Amazon was too delighted with results to take offence. She looked at the needle intently, pressed a button which set an automatic calculator to work, and then she examined the readings. She became puzzled.

'I don't quite understand why the needle should be pointing down instead of up,' she said. 'Atomium exists in outer space in meteorite form, which is where I expect to find it – yet here we have a reading which shows the nearest atomium to 7,200 miles away, to the southwest of this spot. How could that be?'

'You are sure,' Abna asked, 'that this instrument records the nearest atomium, whether it be in large or small quantity?'

'Certainly – and no other can register until the nearer one is removed and put out of the detector's range.'

'Then the explanation is simple. There is atomium on or about the rocket ship from which I rescued you, and which is now lying at the bottom of the Pacific ocean. That is where the recording is coming from.'

'Why, of course!' The Amazon gazed blankly in front of her for a moment. 'When that mass of atomium hit the rocket ship parts of it must have been chipped off and lodged in crevices in the rocket, by which means they were transported back to Earth. That means we've got to fly back to the Pacific immediately – and go down into it with a detector until we locate the stuff.'

'My machine can go under water,' Abna said.

'So can the Ultra – and I prefer to use it. After all, this is my problem more than yours and it would be better if I used my own instruments.'

CHAPTER XII

The Amazon switched on the radio. 'World weather reports may still be being given for the evacuation fliers,' she said. 'If we can get an idea of the conditions we can decide whether to go now or to wait for the weather clearing a little. A few hours won't make much difference.'

The radio came into life in the midst of the midnight bulletin, the weather report due to follow after it.

'. . . and it can only be assumed,' the announcer said, 'that faulty material or some engineering error caused the collapse. Whatever the basic trouble, many people have been trapped by the subsidence and the short-wave radio which the entombed survivors have with them has stated that many well-known people have been killed or seriously injured. Among those badly hurt are Miss Ethel Wilson, the daughter of the space line director for Earth – while those dead include—'

The Amazon switched off, her face bleak. She whirled round on Abna.

'Did you hear that?' she said. 'The very thing I have been fearing! A faulty shelter has collapsed and my foster-niece is one of those injured.' She clenched her fist. 'When I said I would delay dealing with Torrington and his friends until later I made a mistake. I'm going to deal with them now – tonight – once I've discovered how Ethel is. That won't be the only shelter to collapse. Others will follow. Torrington is out to make a fortune from a national calamity. That demands action and my own personal account is overdue.'

'You have thought what it may mean if you appear among the people?' Abna asked. 'You said you wanted to keep away from them.'

'That was before I heard about Ethel.' The Amazon was already hurrying towards the laboratory door. 'What they need is a leader who has their interests at heart. We'll head for the Charing Cross shelter, and since we're going in the Ultra it might be a good idea if you put your machine on top of it. We might need both.'

'I'll do that,' Abna agreed promptly.

'I'll join you as soon as I change into flying kit.'

When the Amazon reappeared she was in a one-piece garment of black with a gold belt about her waist. Abna, turning from surveying his machine secured to the top of the Ultra, smiled as he watched her lithe advance.

'That is how I have mostly seen you attired,' he said. 'When watching you from my home world. We look kinfolk – I in my yellow; you in your black.'

'I've no time to discuss pleasantries,' the Amazon interrupted him. 'Let's be on our way...'

It was only when the Amazon had launched her massive craft into the night – Abna's machine being carried pick-a-back style – that she and the giant beside her realized how frightful were the conditions. The cloud ceiling was zero-zero; the wind velocity 100 m.p.h. as low as 2,000 feet. The blaze of the searchlights from the Ultra's prow only revealed whirling snow and cataracts of frozen rain beating on the impregnable windows.

Inside the warm control cabin, surrounded by the soft glow of the cold-light tubes and the flickering of a multitude of needles on their dials, the two felt no discomfort. Their only consciousness of the inclemency outside lay in the rocking of the vessel as its powerful atom plant drove it from the outskirts of the city to the centre.

To see with the naked eye where they were going was impossible: the infra-screens did it instead. Piercing the night they reflected on to an area in front of the control panel a complete relief map of ice-bound, snow-covered London in the grip of its unnatural Arctic night. There were the deserted streets, dark ghostly buildings, and amidst them all, the bulk around Charing Cross which marked the entrance to the main underground shelter.

'There may be trouble when we land,' she said, glancing up at Abna as he stood beside her. 'Not from the people but from the law officials. They probably know that I am still alive and, if so, they'll have orders to arrest me. We'll deal with that when we come to it.'

Abna nodded. Going over to the storage locker, he opened it and brought forth fur suits. In the few minutes that remained before landing, while the automatic pilot could still be used, he and the Amazon donned them – then once more back at the controls, the girl brought the massive vessel down in the deserted Strand, locked the switchboard by means of a combination lever, and then hurried to the airlock.

Once outside, with small flashlights, she and Abna found themselves battling with a screaming wind and blinding snow. They floundered across the empty space which was Charing Cross and eventually gained the entrance of the station which had become the exterior section of London's chief shelter.

The big metal doors of the place were closed, white barriers in the snow. Raising her gloved hands, the Amazon pounded heavily, and Abna did likewise. Finally a slide moved up at eye level, a slide with a two-inch thick glass. A face was visible beyond and a voice spoke by loudspeaker system.

'Who is it? Identify yourselves.'

'Refugees,' the Amazon answered. 'For heaven's sake let us in!'

'Names?' the guard insisted. 'I must have your names and check them with the index—'

The Amazon reflected swiftly, trying to think of two names which would do the trick. Abna, however, acted otherwise. Raising his huge gloved hand he drove it suddenly with shattering power into the glass panel. The blow went through the two-inch thickness, showering glass on the astounded guard. He was even more astounded when the gloved hand seized him by the throat and fingers tightened with terrifying power.

'Open the door!' Abna commanded. 'And do it now!'

The guard struggled and writhed, but the more he did so the more the gloved hand tightened remorselessly on his windpipe. At last, gasping, he pulled an automatic switch and the twin doors rumbled slowly apart. Immediately Abna released his hold and he and the Amazon darted into the vast interior of what had once been a railroad station.

Now the entire area was brightly lighted, the space taken up by the hundreds of clerks and similar workers who had to deal with the shelter's inmates. In the distance, the stairs which had led to the underground railway had been altered in design and over the top of each were directions concerning to which shelter each stairway led.

'What about your names?' the guard insisted. 'I must have them!'

'You can have mine, anyway,' the Amazon replied curtly, tossing aside her hood and face mask. 'Or is that necessary?'

The guard stared at her cynical face, the glint in her violet eyes, the tumbled masses of her golden hair.

'The – the Amazon! I didn't—'

Suddenly his hand flashed down to the weapon he was carrying but before he had completed the action Abna slammed out his left fist. It lifted the guard straight off his feet, and he dropped on his face and stayed there.

The Amazon said: 'I thought it would be known that I had returned.' Her hand whipped inside her fur suit and yanked a proton gun from her belt. She levelled it at the clerical staff as she advanced toward it.

'I'm not here just for the fun of it or to pass the night,' she stated. 'Whereabouts is the shelter which has fallen in and buried Miss Wilson? Hurry up, somebody – answer!'

'Th-there,' one of the girl clerks stammered, pointing to the central stairway which had been converted. 'And Miss Brant—' she ventured as the Amazon swung away.

'Well?' The Amazon looked back over her shoulder, Abna beside her, lowering his face mask.

'I'd like you to know that we don't all feel against you – like that guard. We'd like you back, especially at a time like this—'

'Save it till later,' the Amazon interrupted.

She motioned Abna and together they hurried to the opening of the one-time stairway the girl had indicated. Part of it indeed still was a staircase of the escalator type. It bore the two down into the brightly lighted underworld. When they had descended 500 feet down a shaft lined with gleaming metal they came upon the underworld refuge they were seeking.

From end to end it was packed with men, women and children. Some were on the move with their belongings; others were sitting brooding – and to the left, a group was busy with electric drills. The Amazon hurried toward them, and the people, recognizing her, fell back a little at her approach.

'Is this where the collapse is?' she demanded of the engineer in charge.

The engineer's face lighted at the sight of his questioner.

'Then it was true!' he ejaculated. 'You're still alive, Miss Brant! Thank heaven for that!'

'Obviously I'm alive,' she said irritably. 'Answer my question.'

'Yes, this is where we're trying to get through,' the engineer agreed. 'It's a bad fall – Look for yourself.'

The Amazon was already looking. Where there should have been another shaft leading to lower caverns there was instead a large area of crushed metal plates, twisted stanchions, and crumbled rock. The whole shaft at this point had apparently gone rotten and caved in.

'What happened?' she asked.

'Simply folded up,' the engineer shrugged. 'The folks in the lower cavern were buried. The moving staircase was smashed to bits as well; you can see parts of it there sticking up. Some of the people survived but quite a few are hurt. We're in touch by radio and in another hour we ought to have got to them—'

'We'll help,' the Amazon said quickly, stepping out of her furs. 'You, too, Abna.'

'Willingly,' Abna agreed, and flung his fur suit aside.

CHAPTER XIII

The engineer and his fellow technicians stared in wonder for a moment at the mightily muscled stranger; then pressure of events forced them to work again. But this time it was the Amazon who gave the directions, not the chief engineer – and he was content to relinquish himself to her greater knowledge.

Whirring and grinding, the atomic drills bit gradually through the debris while the men and the Amazon hurled aside the heavy material which the multiple excavators could not easily grasp.

So, within 40 minutes a passage through the rock and rubble had been bored. The Amazon was the first to squeeze down through the narrow space and drop into the cavern below. Here she found about 100 people. The metal walls sagged dangerously around them, the only light they possessed coming from the batteries with which they had been operating their radio.

The Amazon glanced over the assembly swiftly, then her gaze moved to those who were lying flat, their relatives or friends kneeling beside them.

'Chris!' the Amazon exclaimed suddenly, and hurried over to the dirt-streaked man kneeling beside Ethel. Ethel herself, motionless, her face blood-smeared, was muttering incoherently.

'She's dying, Vi,' Chris whispered. He was too stunned by the events to ask any questions of her reason for being present. 'She got crushed in the rocks. Can't last much longer.'

The Amazon glanced about her. Chris interpreted the action.

'My wife is in one of the other caverns,' he said. 'Quite safe so far.'

The Amazon got up from her knees as Abna and the engineers, followed by others from the upper cavern, came down into view.

'Listen, you people,' she said, raising her voice. 'You can think of me as you like, but it is an undeniable fact that many of you may yet die if you don't follow me from here on and ignore whatever other orders you may have been given. These shelters are rotten! They have got to be rebuilt before it's too late. How many of you are prepared to throw Torrington's lying propaganda overboard and follow me?'

'All of us!' a man yelled. 'We never did believe that big-mouthed money-bags anyway!'

'All right, then. Here are your first orders. Get everybody possible up to the higher cavern and there stop for the time being. Issue radio instructions for all those in deep caverns to come as near the surface as possible. Now give me a hand to get the injured out of here. I'll deal with Miss Wilson; you folks look after the others.'

The Amazon returned to Ethel's side and caught at the girl's hand. For a moment Ethel's incoherency seemed to leave her and she gazed into the steady violet eyes dully.

'Hello – Aunt Vi,' she whispered. 'It's nice to know you're around again. Nobody but you can get things straight. I'm finished, Aunt...'

The Amazon pulled down the overcoat which Chris had thrown over the girl's legs. She wondered how Ethel came to be alive at all, so mercilessly had the rocks crushed her legs and body.

'May I look?' asked Abna quietly.

The Amazon glanced up. Ethel opened her eyes again at the new voice. For a second or two wonder overcame her agony.

'What – what a man!' she breathed. 'If only—' She broke off, her face contorted with pain.

'Is this business beyond you, Miss Brant?' Abna murmured in the Amazon's ear.

'I'm afraid it is. If only I had surgical instruments handy I could save her. It can't be done otherwise. She can't live long.'

'I have seen and cured worse than this.'

The Amazon stared, and so did Chris.

'Whatever you can do, Abna, do,' the Amazon urged. 'She means a lot to me – more than I can explain. As if she were my own daughter.'

Abna nodded; then suddenly a queer change of expression

came over him as he gazed at Ethel. A look of tremendous intentness came on his handsome features, while his reddish-blue eyes became fixed and unblinking. He raised Ethel's slim shoulders and forced her to look at him.

'Don't speak, Miss Wilson,' he said gently. 'Just look at me, that's all.'

Ethel obeyed, and motionless, the Amazon, Chris, and the others still in the cavern watched. As far as they could tell, something like a miracle was being enacted before their very eyes – for, gradually, as Ethel remained rigid, her eyes staring into Abna's, her crushed legs began to heal and fill out. The flow of blood ceased. Smooth skin appeared. Like a slow transformation in a movie she gradually became her normal figure again, was as unhurt as though she had never been touched.

'There,' Abna murmured finally, smiling and lowering his hands. 'That feel better, young lady?'

Ethel blinked, passed a hand over her forehead, and then looked down at herself.

'In heaven's name what did you do?' she gasped. 'Who are you? A healer or something?'

'Not in the sense that you mean it,' Abna responded. 'I am a scientist, the same as Miss Brant, but my science is of another order. We of my planet – which you call Jupiter – believe that any material thing is grosser than the mental state, therefore the mental power can force the material to obey it. That was what happened. By mind force I made you see yourself as you were before your accident. Your physical frame was compelled to yield to your mental outlook and . . . Well, you are as sound as ever.'

Ethel got slowly on to her feet, her jaw sagging. 'It's – it's much too deep for me,' she confessed, staring up at her deliverer.

'Then just forget it,' he suggested. 'I'm glad I was able to help you.'

'You expect us to forget such a thing!' Chris exclaimed, gripping Abna's hand in gratitude. 'You have a queer idea of our mentality on this world, Abna!'

'I have a great respect for it. Most of it, anyway,' Abna responded.

'I just can't begin to say anything,' Ethel muttered, her eyes fixed on the giant in girlish fascination. 'My father did tell me about you, Mr. Abna – what kind of a wonder-man you are, but I never expected anybody like you!'

'We're wasting time,' the Amazon said abruptly. 'Abna, you are better able to deal with these injured people than I am, so I'm going to get busy with other matters. Since I am taking control it means that Torrington and his money grabbers have no place in the scheme of things. I'll be back,' she added, and turned away.

In a few minutes she had clambered out of the lower cavern, pushing her way through the people. After a while she gained the side of the chief engineer who, with his men, was still labouring to make the shaft wider.

'Where can I find Torrington?' she asked.

'He has his headquarters over there.' The engineer nodded across the great space to a remote door.

'Trust him to choose a place where no subsidence can affect him,' the Amazon murmured, her eyes gleaming. 'All right – thanks. And henceforth you're taking your orders from me.'

'Suits me,' the engineer agreed.

CHAPTER XIV

The Amazon made her way swiftly through the throngs of people, reached the door in the metal wall inscribed 'Headquarters – Strictly Private', and hammered forcibly on it. After a brief while it opened and an official in uniform appeared.

'Well?' he snapped, his hand on his gun – then he suddenly realized whom he was addressing.

'Don't waste your time doing that,' the Amazon warned, whipping her own gun from her belt. 'Take me to Torrington.'

He nodded and closed the door. The Amazon followed him across an expansive, comfortably furnished area. Torrington and his cohorts had certainly taken care that they would endure no hardships.

At one of the many doors lining the walls the guard stopped and knocked timidly. There was no response.

'Here, let me do it!' the Amazon ripped the guard's gun from his belt, threw it away, and then gave him a shove which sent him sprawling. Turning to the door, she hammered violently upon it, still received no answer, and so turned her proton gun on it. There was a transient blinding flame and the dispersal of acrid fumes. A kick sent the door swinging inward, and the Amazon stood on the threshold, staring into gloom.

She stepped quickly into the dark and to one side, preventing herself being a silhouette against the light of the adjoining room. Almost at the identical moment a gun blazed out of the dark and the bullet whanged close to her face.

'Evidently you were expecting me, Torrington,' she commented.

Her eyes, accustomed by now to the abrupt change, had the gift of seeing in the dark. She could descry the dim outline of a figure crouched behind a big chair, the light catching his gun. He was peering blindly into the gloom, apparently trying to take aim.

Swiftly as a tigress the Amazon crossed the room, whirled the chair to one side, and was upon the startled tycoon before he realized what had happened. Now in the dim reflected light from the chamber beyond he could see the girl's merciless face. A steel grip on his wrist flung the revolver from his hand; a blow in the jaw knocked him reeling. With a heavy impact he crashed back against the wall.

The Amazon returned to the door, shut it as best she could with its broken lock, and then snapped on the light. Smiling coldly, she gazed at the metals king as he crouched by the far wall, his hair dishevelled, terror in his eyes.

'Just what are you planning to do, Amazon? I know you think that I was responsible for you being fired into space – but it was the wish of the people and the edict of the court.'

The Amazon began to move forward slowly. 'There is no place for you in my plans, nor for those avaricious apes who have helped you. I mean Arnside and Swainson. I warned you that one day I'd take care of you all – and that is what I mean to do. Now get Arnside and Swainson.'

'I don't know where they are?' Torrington objected.

'Don't lie! Find them!'

'That shouldn't be difficult,' a voice commented quietly, right behind the Amazon. 'And drop that gun, Miss Brant!'

Something hard dug in her back. She dropped her weapon, raised her hands, and turned, Morris Arnside and Swainson were considering her, both of them with revolvers. They had evidently crept in from the outer room and entered soundlessly.

'Now,' Arnside commented, 'what did you want with us, Miss Brant? Or is it more to the point what we want with you? From what I can gather, you have decided to upset the Triumvirate, which is the government of we three men until the solar crisis has passed.'

A surprised look crossed the Amazon's face. 'So that's it!' she ejaculated. 'You are fools enough to think that one day the sun will recover and you will be able to spend your blood money? I wondered why you were so anxious to make your fortunes out of a catastrophe.'

'Certainly the sun will recover,' Torrington stated. 'I am convinced of it – and without help from you. In fact I don't think you'll be around to see that recovery or any other.' He motioned. 'Arnside, there's some strong sash cord over there in that cupboard. Get it and tie her up. We can get rid of her through the shaft trap in the next room.'

Arnside nodded and turned away, leaving only Swainson with his levelled gun, and the Amazon made a tremendous leap and flattened Swainson to the floor.

Arnside twirled, his gun in his hand, but in a flying tackle the Amazon had reached him, her arms locked around his leg. He crashed over, half rose, then sagged again before a blow in the face which smashed his nose.

'This sort of horseplay won't do you much good,' Torrington panted, his own gun now recovered and ready in his hand. 'Get up, Amazon, and stand over there!'

She obeyed, but with one hand she dragged up Arnside's limp body with her, holding him by the jacket collar. In so doing she covered herself against Torrington's gun. He twisted to one side to aim again, but did not have the opportunity. Suddenly Arnside's flailing body hurled through the air, cannoned into the metals king, and knocked him sprawling. Winded and dazed, he flung Arnside's body away from him, only to find another one pinning him. A black-clad knee was jammed in his chest and fingers with the grip of steel pliers sank deep into his fleshy neck.

'You had no mercy on me, Torrington, or upon the people who met death and injury in your rotten shelters,' the Amazon murmured. 'So I'm going to kill you – as you deserve to be killed.'

He tore at the black-clad forearms reaching down to him. He punched and kicked and writhed but failed completely to dislodge the grip on his throat.

The Amazon relaxed at last and contemplated the body. Then with a gesture of contempt she got to her feet and looked at the other two men. To her surprise she found on examination that Swainson was also dead. The smashing blow she had delivered on his neck had broken it. Only Arnside still lived, groaning slowly into consciousness. Reaching down, the Amazon whirled him to his feet and then pinned him hard against the wall with one hand at his throat.

'Listen to me, Arnside—!' She slapped his face until he came back to awareness. 'You remain alive out of three. I could kill you – and indeed enjoy it – but I think you are too insignificant to bother with. You had great dreams and thought Torrington could make them come true. Forget them and henceforth do as I order. If you don't, I'll finish you . . . That's all!'

She released him and he stood fingering his smashed nose and looking at her. Then she picked up her proton gun, returned it to her belt, and sped to the open doorway. Just at that moment Abna came in with Chris Wilson and Ethel behind him. He gazed about the headquarters.

'Dead?' he inquired, looking at Swainson and then Torrington.

'Yes.' The Amazon shrugged. 'They deserved it. They got it. That has always been my code.'

'It has the merit of being thorough,' Abna commented, musing. 'And what do you propose doing now?'

'Since I have made myself the leader I propose spending the next few hours getting order out of chaos and having the shelters up and down the country tested and put to rights. It will be hard going and I shall need every trustworthy lieutenant I can find. You will be my right-hand man, Abna, then will come you, Chris! you Rosy—'

'And my wife,' Chris interrupted. 'She's okay, I found out that much. She'll be joining us shortly.'

'All right.' The Amazon glanced over the room again. 'This may as well remain headquarters. Summon the engineers and all those engaged on the shelter work – and the head of the clerical staff. We'll hold a conference. After that, Abna and I have a journey to make to the Pacific.'

After all the equipment of her laboratory had been transferred to the shelter, the Amazon threw herself into her task with all the terrific energy of which she was capable, immediately after she had held a conference and worked out details.

She worked so furiously that Chris, his wife and Ethel just could not keep up with her. She refused to sleep; she brooded over plans, worked out new schemes, had shelters tested in all parts of the country and the reports sent to her – then fresh instructions went out to the blast furnaces which were working underground. She and Abna devised a new metal for protection, one capable of withstanding the vast pressure of the Great Glacier when it finally came.

Instead of several separate shafts, one alone was decided upon. Going down two miles into the earth to virgin rock, was to be one huge underground city, having all the amenities and facilities of a surface city. At the top of the shaft would be a transparent dome, fitted with defreezing devices which would prevent the glacier from forming on top of it, thereby permitting of ingress and egress if journeys into the outer world became necessary.

Tests had shown that the metal with which the shaft was to be made, and the glass for the dome, could withstand a direct pressure of 15,000,000 tons to the square inch without cracking. Only when this perfection was reached did the Amazon pass the metal for manufacture in vast quantities.

It took two days to make the plans and test the metals, using every scientific device – then the actual work began, every able-bodied person being pressed into commission. As far as could be the actual planning was complete. Whether or not the shaft and underworld could be finished before the glacier came was something nobody could forecast. Working to the limit of human endurance it might just be managed.

So, finally, after a week of tireless endeavour, the Amazon felt reasonably satisfied that she had done all she could. The rest was up to the unswerving and prompt execution of her orders and the supervision of the engineers under her command. For a week she had not slept and only eaten tabloids and drunk restoratives when necessity had compelled it. She was commencing to feel the strain. It was visible in her lined face and the weary smile she gave Abna as he sat beside her at the big desk in the headquarters office.

'You need sleep,' he told her, 'before anything further is attempted.'

She sighed. 'Sleep! What time is there for that! Don't you realize that if we're unable to find atomium and develop it for use within the next few weeks it may be too late? By then the last spark will have gone out of the sun and we'll be doomed to stay below here for ever.'

'I realize it,' Abna responded. 'And I also realize that you need sleep.'

'Don't you need it as well?' the girl questioned. 'You have worked ceaselessly beside me, and by rights ought to be feeling the effects as much as I am. I can stand a good deal but I do know my limits.'

Abna considered her tired face and smiled. 'I know you do. That is one of the many things I like about you. It satisfies me that you are still a woman underneath the exterior of super-human power and intelligence. I could never be interested in a woman who is just a sexless machine,' he finished. 'The world has done you a great injustice in calling you that.'

'I asked,' the Amazon questioned deliberately, 'whether or not you feel tired.'

'No, I don't. Like the rest of my race I have trained my mind to control my body. I could only feel tired if my mind was tired – and it is not.'

Abna got to his feet, then before the Amazon could gather his intentions he picked her up from the chair and bore her into the adjoining room which she was using as her own. He laid her down gently on the bed and smiled.

'I'll call you when I think you have rested enough,' he said. 'In the meantime I'll see that the Ultra is in order – with atomium-detector aboard – for our Pacific journey, together with all other preparations—'

'But you don't know anything about the Ultra!' the Amazon exclaimed.

'I know more than you think. Please rest. You need it.'

The Amazon hesitated, still not sure whether or not she had been commanded to sleep – in which case, on principle, she would have tried to keep awake – or whether Abna was genuinely solicitous for her well-being. She was still trying to figure the business out when drowsiness overtook her and she relaxed, losing herself in dreams.

The young giant beside her stood for a few minutes contemplating her earnestly, considering the beauty of her face even in sleep, the sensitive amber-tinted hands, limply relaxed, giving no hint of the power they possessed.

'Yes . . .' he murmured finally. 'You are the woman.'

He straightened up, switched off the light, and went to ask Chris Wilson to come to the headquarters office.

'Frankly, Mr. Wilson, I want a few facts, and you are the best man to give them to me,' he said.

'Willingly, if I can.'

'Tell me then about Miss Brant. I know her life history as far as records and public reports have given it – but I would like to know everything. I think you will agree she is not the kind of woman to answer of her own volition, so I am asking you.'

'Before I do,' Chris said, 'please answer me a question. Are you in love with Vi – Miss Brant?'

'I am. I loved her when I first saw her through our telescopic equipment. My feeling about her is that she and I would make a perfect union. But what worries me is that if she is as sexless as records paint her she will never have any regard for me.'

'Now I understand,' Chris said. 'You can discount such nonsense—'

'Not very easily, I am afraid. She is a supernormal female member of your community. Her entire structure was altered by that Dr. Axton when she was but three years of age. What guarantee is there that he did not render her as sexless as records claim?'

'I believe,' Chris answered, 'that Vi is as much a woman as any other member of her sex. In my long association with her I have been aware of her hatred of men, of course, but it has been a hatred directed against men who have deserved it. Her contempt for men has been because on the one hand she had never met a man capable of standing up to her either physically or mentally; and also because she has an intensely individual character, complete unto itself. But I have seen times when there has been tenderness in her make-up – even a great loneliness which has probably made her far more cruel than she would otherwise have been. She knows she is not a natural woman and at times I think she rebels against it. 'But', Chris finished. 'I'd stake everything I've got that a man like you is just the kind of partner she needs.'

Abna said, 'I have a plan in mind, Mr. Wilson. The union of myself and Miss Brant – marriage as you call it – would be a wonderful thing, but it would only make us legal partners pursuing scientific aims far above the normal ken of people on this planet. If though, there were children . . . Did you ever stop to think what the children of two such people as Miss Brant and myself might be like?'

Chris shrugged. 'It never occured to me – but my imagination is not so limited that I cannot help but foresee a race of supermen and women in time.'

'Who in time would inherit the earth,' Abna said. 'That is part of my dream, Mr. Wilson, which one day I shall hope to discuss with Miss Brant herself. It can never succeed if there are never any children. Did Dr. Axton, in his experiment, have the unparalleled cruelty to render Miss Brant incapable of bearing children?'

'According to the reports I have seen, which Miss Brant herself once showed my wife and me, no,' Chris replied. 'Axton gave her great beauty, immense strength and almost eternal life – but there he stopped. Axton, my friend, was not a devil. He was a surgical genius who wanted to improve the world. He would never have destroyed the birthright of a child.'

'Thank you.' Abna got to his feet, and with his arm about the smaller man's shoulder, walked to the door. 'I'm grateful to you, Mr. Wilson.'

Chris said: 'I have many a time suggested to her that she find a partner, and been laughed at for my trouble. I think she loves children in her own possessive way. Certainly she is profoundly fond of Ethel, my daughter, and always has been. You saw how she reacted when she thought Ethel was in danger of dying.'

'I still remember her words,' Abna responded. 'She said, "I look upon her as though she were my own daughter." A woman with no womanly feeling would never have said that.'

CHAPTER XV

The Amazon awoke as her shoulder was shaken gently. She was conscious upon opening her eyes of feeling greatly rested in mind and body. Her gaze rested on Abna. He had a tray in his hands and upon it a meal.

'Breakfast in bed!' the Amazon asked drily, propping herself up on her elbow. 'How little you know me yet!'

'Have it just the same,' he suggested, pulling up a chair.

There seemed to be no point in arguing, so the Amazon began the meal and took the drink he poured out and handed to her. After a while she glanced at the clock.

'Eleven . . . At night or in the morning?' she asked.

'Morning. You've been asleep for 48 hours.'

The Amazon sighed. 'Then I'm losing my grip! I never slept so long in my life before.'

'Perhaps you never worked so hard in your life before. I have everything prepared for the Pacific flight,' Abna continued, before she could comment further. 'We are not going to have an easy time, either. The Pacific is freezing over, according to reports, and it will be touch and go whether the part we want is clear of ice or not. However, I notice your Ultra has protonic gun equipment and heat beams so we should overcome our difficulties.'

'We will,' she assured him, in her old, confident tone. 'What of the Great Glacier? How far away is it?'

'It has reached North Scotland and is travelling steadily south. The latest bolometer reading of the sun puts his temperature as 2,500 centigrade and still dropping. He has turned from yellow to red, the penultimate stage of devolution before he comes to the dark star range. We've a fight on our hands, Vi.'

At the mention of her first name which Abna had never before used, the Amazon looked at him with her steady violet eyes.

'Is Abna your first or second name?' she asked abruptly.

'Both. Atlantean names are mostly single. The name of the

progenitor. I hope you are not offended at my using your own first name?'

'On the contrary. I was wondering when you were going to.' The Amazon smiled a little, met the calm scrutiny in his eyes, and then brought her refreshment to a hurried close.

'Freshen up, and then join me in the headquarters office,' Abna said. 'You'll need the heaviest furs you've got.'

When later they left the underworld the Amazon found it hard to believe that they were still on the same planet. On the other side of the barrier the world had, to the Amazon, anyway, changed incredibly in the past week.

The snow had frozen solid and to glasslike hardness. She and Abna moved clumsily in their heavy fur wrappings, floundering up the slope which led from the doors, and so reaching what had been the snow-covered expanse outside the station. Now it was one sheet of ice.

It was high noon, and as dark as a winter's dawn! For the moment there was no blizzard; not even a cloud. London, and probably the whole world, had become a wilderness in the past 10 days – a terrifying wilderness in which no living thing moved. The sun, a deep red with neither heat nor light, the globe spotted with chasms which were eating away his life. Dim, hardly visible, loomed the moon. Only the stars were alive – brilliant, winking, spared the fate of their doomed brother.

'Grim, isn't it?' Abna asked, through the audiphone which connected him with the Amazon's helmet.

'It will be still grimmer if we don't act fast,' she responded, as they went on again. 'The cold now is pretty nearly equal to that of outer space. Nothing can live on the surface any more. I've imagined what the death of the sun might look like, but in my wildest imagining I never thought of this.'

Before they reached the Ultra – from which Abna had removed his own flier and housed it in the shelter – the calmness had gone. A blizzard developed with incredible speed, swallowing up the heavens in surging clouds and driving before it blinding sheets of powdered ice and snow. The screaming wind bit deep, even through the protective furs.

Struggling on like two Arctic explorers, Abna and the

Amazon continued moving until at last the Ultra, poised high atop a glassy ridge, loomed dimly before them. They struggled with the airlock, their big gloves hindering their movements, but finally they got it open. Thankfully they tumbled into the control room and slammed the heavy operculum shut behind them.

'I suppose,' Abna said, switching on the lights and the auto-heater, 'that you and I, Vi, should be glad that we are not as other men and women – that we have the endurance to carry on. Ordinary human beings would never be able to make the fight we are making.'

The Amazon tugged off her furs and Abna did likewise. He found her looking at him quizzically.

'You never forget to mention how alike we are in physical power and interests, do you?' she questioned.

He smiled but made no comment. The Amazon shrugged, turned aside, and settled at the control board. Abna moved to her side and nodded to the navigational map.

'I worked it out in advance to save time,' he explained. 'We should be able to fly straight to the spot.'

The Amazon nodded. There seemed to be no point in questioning Abna's knowledge. Apparently he had learned all there was to learn about the Ultra. She switched on the atomic power plant, then moved the switches. With a grinding roar the vessel tore free of the imprisoning grip of ice about her base and nosed up in an almost vertical ascent. The storm area persisted for many thousands of feet, a belt of tremendous upheavals far greater than anything the Amazon had ever experienced.

Then suddenly the storm area had been left behind – but instead of the accustomed blaze of the sun at those vast heights there was only a glitter of the stars and the burned-out hulk of the lord of the day.

The Amazon stopped the Ultra's climb and turned the vessel south-westward, gradually building up to the maximum air speed of 5,000 miles an hour, cleaving through the attenuated gulf at the very edge of the stratosphere with the black maw of the unnatural dark infinitely far below.

When the Caribbean was reached the clouds had thinned

and there was a view of frozen sea, with tiny specks of vessels crushed in its remoreless jaws. The West Indies and Central America lay under a blanket of ice; and so onward to the Pacific, and then a southerly turn. Here again all was ice.

'We should start going down now,' Abna said, studying his atomium detector. 'The needle's pointing almost directly below us.'

The Amazon who had been watching the instruments at intervals, began to dip the machine's nose, sweeping down with tremendous velocity from the airless heights to the region of snow clouds once more. She flew the Ultra low over the icy wilderness which was the Pacific ocean; then she began to circle the vessel until she had reached the point where the atomium detector needle gave the exact downward reading.

'Heat beams!' she cried.

Abna was already at the projectors, and he snapped the instruments on. Invisible radiation of the equivalent wave-length of intense heat stabbed down into the ice field. Steam rose. The ice cracked and then melted, until finally it was boiling. Slowly, with the machine circling, Abna cut out a big cleft in the ice and the Amazon sent the Ultra diving into it.

Lower the Ultra sank and lower. Half a mile – one mile – a mile and a half. Down here the cold of the surface had not yet reached and fish were not affected. Gulper eels, with their vast mouths, were fairly common; then came the Giant Lantern fish, the Black Swallower, the Constellation fish – all of them known to science. But as the Ultra went still lower, fish were rare, but now and again lights did pick out incomprehensible shapes, huge beyond imagination, prehistoric monsters of the deep, so built that they would withstand the terrific pressures existing at this depth. And it was this thought of pressures which presently caused the Amazon to glance about her in some anxiety.

'What is it?' Abna questioned.

'I'm thinking of the risk we're taking. This machine is not made to stand vast pressure. It's for space travel where there is no pressure worth mentioning. If the plates should cave in, we'll be finished!'

'They won't,' Abna replied. 'While you slept, I had the Ultra sheathed in metal of the same type we're using for the shelters, capable of withstanding enormous pressure. When I said I had made all preparations I meant it.'

The Amazon relaxed again, a half smile curving her lips.

'You accomplish the most extraordinary feats in the most matter-of-fact way,' she said. 'That is one of the qualities I admire in you, Abna.'

'I hope there are others, too,' he murmured.

The Amazon did not continue the topic. She kept on, nosing the Ultra down into the depths, farther than any living beings had ever explored before – and still those fantastic shapes, against which whales would have been mere shrimps, occasionally drifted in the still, deadly silent world.

'Four and a half miles down,' Abna said at last. 'That must be about the limit at this point of the ocean—'

He had scarcely completed his sentence before there was a bump and the Ultra seemed to bounce. A thick, oily ooze surged up around the windows, disturbed by the vessel's plunge into the seabed. When it had cleared, the Amazon and Abna stared intently into the space illuminated by the searchlights.

'There it is!' Abna said abruptly, pointing. 'The remains of that rocket ship.'

The Amazon saw it at the same moment, a framework of metal, its plates buckled and bent from the water pressure, its nose half buried in the oozing sand.

'Easier than we expected,' she commented thankfully. 'All we want on it are magnetic grapples and we'll take it back to the surface.'

She switched on the magnetic grapples connected to the power plant and the power-bar hummed with the energy passing through it and the strain entailed. Gradually, drawn irresistibly, the hulk tore free of the ocean bed and attached itself to the magnets.

'Up we go,' the Amazon murmured, and snapped in the switches.

The effect now was that the recoil apparatus pushed the vessel upward, helped by its natural buoyancy, where formerly it had been operating in the opposite direction – against the mass of water – thrusting the vessel down.

CHAPTER XVI

Suddenly there was a violent jolting. It was so severe it nearly knocked them from their feet. At the same instant the power plant whined dangerously, a sure sign that a great amount of energy was being squandered to no purpose, and with the accompanying danger of a power burn-out.

The Amazon flung herself to the outlook window, and, seizing the searchlight controls, swung the beam around outside. As she did so the floor heaved and rocked so violently that she could hardly stay on her feet.

'It's a fish!' she gasped at last. 'As big as a cathedral! Just look at the thing!'

Abna stumbled over to her side and stared out at a sea denizen so vast it was nearly incredible. Evidently it belonged to a class of sea monster long since banished from the Earth. Whatever it was, for its bulk was so enormous as to be shapeless, the 500-foot long Ultra was small by comparison and at the moment was in the thing's vast jaws, the rocking being caused by the fish's motion as it travelled through the depths.

The Amazon said: 'The protonic gun should blow it to pieces – its head anyway, and that's the part that's annoying us.'

He joined her at the switchboard controlling the weapon. To focus the gun on the yawning roof of the giant's mouth was only a moment's work; then the buttons were pressed.

The monster was only wounded and it threshed about with inconceivable savagery, whirling the Ultra around in its mighty jaws until Abna and the Amazon were flung from the gun and pitched helplessly up and down on the floor and against the walls.

Outside the vessel the jutting noses of the proton guns were snapped off against the creature's triple rows of teeth, rendering the weapon useless – a fact which soon became evident to Abna when, struggling to his feet, he tried the guns again.

'Only one thing for it,' he said. 'We'll have to put on every scrap of power we've got and try to drag her free. If we don't, this thing may take us to some lair from which we'll never escape. If he exerts enough pressure he'll crack the vessel.'

With the control cabin gyrating wildly around him, Abna lurched to the driving panel and moved the power levers. The already whining plant began to shriek as with every bolt of its available energy the Ultra strove to tear loose. Fascinated, the Amazon stared out of the window, watching results, clinging to the wall stanchions to save herself being thrown over.

The Ultra jerked, evidently having torn loose from part of the monster's grip. Then for 15 minutes it was a tug-of-war between the giant's teeth and the atom plant.

Throughout the time the power plant shrieked its song of defiance, radiating a drenching heat and turning the air stale. Time and again the monster felt his prize slipping and again tightened his hold. It was like a determined terrier swinging by his teeth to a gradually slipping leash. But slowly the monster began to tire, partly because of the wounds he had received which no doubt made his grip less deadly than it would otherwise have been.

Then came a moment when at last the straining Ultra ripped clear, so suddenly it seemed to bounce. The swaying and gyrations ceased and the horrific monster of the deep was lost in his own abysmal region.

'Thank heaven,' the Amazon whispered, heaving a sigh. 'And I hope we meet no more of them! The rocket ship's still safely anchored,' she added, peering obliquely out of the window.

'We ought to be able to—'

Abna paused and exchanged a startled look with the girl. For the noise of the power plant had ceased and there was a complete, unnatural quiet.

Together they moved to the nerve centre of the vessel, expecting to find some part of the motor had been burned out under the excessive demands which had been made upon it. Instead they beheld the jaws of the main bar pressed tightly together with no copper block between.

'We're out of fuel!' the Amazon said blankly. 'The power bar's been completely consumed. It must have been in our struggle with that fish. I have no spare power bars either. I never thought they would be needed. There was enough energy in that bar to carry us to Mars and back.'

'We overlooked a point,' Abna said. 'Flying to Mars demands hardly any power beyond the initial take-off. In outer space there is no retardation, but here we fight resistance every inch of the way.'

He went to the control board and studied the meters and gauges. He turned. 'We're motionless,' he said. 'Neither rising nor descending. I should have thought our buoyancy would have carried us up—'

'So it should,' the Amazon insisted, staring out of the window, 'but not while that holds us.' Abna saw what she meant. The vessel was ensnared in a filigree of unidentifiable water vegetation, its roots evidently in the sea bed. Normally the vessel would have ripped through it with ease, but now, without power; it was caught.

'There's only one way,' Abna said at last, and the girl looked at him hopefully.

'We must dismantle everything we can,' he said, 'and use it in the power plant. Pure copper is the best medium, but everything that has atomic energy. We shall also lighten the load in the ship. All the instruments, the guns, everything we can find must be converted into energy. The pity is that atomium can only release its energy under the influence of a fixed supersonic vibration, otherwise we could use that.'

For the next half hour they behaved pretty much like vandals, tearing away everything metallic that was not immediately needful and throwing it on the floor in a pile. It made the Amazon wince to have to dismantle much of her valuable apparatus for scrap, but it had to be done. Even several stanchion bars were unbolted. These, together with the pile of smaller objects, Abna fixed between the jaws of the power plant and then switched on the current. Immediately the mass of metal began to glow and shrink slightly, but the Ultra jolted, swerved, and then restarted its ascent to the surface.

Throughout the trip the Amazon kept her gaze anxiously on the fast consuming material. Not being copper, or even intended for the purpose of providing atomic energy, the metal evaporated at an alarming speed. Only a small residue was left by the time the Ultra had finished its ascent and struck hard against the underside of the ice. Abna, who had been controlling the vessel, switched off the power and stood thinking.

'How thick this ice is we don't know,' he said at length, 'and the heat beams are fed from the power plant. Do you suppose we have enough stuff left to get through?'

'We've got to,' the Amazon responded. 'Let's see what else we can part with.'

The storage cupboards were taken to pieces, together with the metal shelves. The stands for the protonic guns were dismantled. Whole sections of the switchboard with its basically metal material were sacrificed – until at last it seemed there was enough. The material was fed to the power plant and the current switched on again.

This time the girl took the controls while Abna directed the heat beams. The underside of the ice began to melt under the vibration and an ever-widening chasm started to appear, boiling where the furious heat struck it and expanding into battered clouds of steam. Slowly, through dense, foggy water, the Ultra began to move up, walls of ice sliding past in the process.

How long it took to penetrate the barrier neither the Amazon nor Abna noticed. They were too intent on either watching the diminishing fuel or else the riven path ahead. This was the critical time, for if the power failed now, the ice would reform, expand by natural law, and crush the Ultra like an egg shell before any more scrap could be found. As it was, the plant was labouring at times, struggling with the double task of providing the heat beams with energy and forcing the vessel upward.

Then the Amazon suddenly gave a cry of delight.

'We're through, Abna! We've made it!'

He smiled in relief. The Ultra had split the last skin of ice and with a mighty surge it now leaped clear and into the air as the Amazon made a lightning change in the controls. Gone was all the pressure as the vessel climbed ever faster into the dark mid-afternoon sky, with its ghost of a sun and myriad glittering stars. The whine of the power plant dropped to its normal humming.

'Just about enough fuel to reach London,' Abna said, contemplating the atom plant's jaws.

He was right. The last pieces of metal were vapourizing as the Ultra came within sight of the frozen city and swept down to the ice outside the shelter's massive doors. The Amazon switched off, and they got into their fur suits, and then she opened the airlock.

'Best thing we can do is drive the Ultra into the shelter,' she said. 'Left out here it will either be frozen in or crushed under the Great Glacier when it comes. We shall have to re-equip everything we've pulled to pieces, too.'

Abna nodded and followed her out into the biting air.

CHAPTER XVII

Two hours later the inhabitants of the shelter were in possession of the facts of the desperate journey to the ocean's depths; then the Amazon and Abna retired to the laboratory at the second shelter level. Here, behind closed doors, they went to work to examine the hulk of the rocket flier and the atomium that had lodged on it.

Their search took them four hours, and when they had completed it they had upon the testing bench about four ounces of granular grey material remarkably like coke but of tremendous heaviness.

'How do you suppose we can test it?' the Amazon inquired. 'If we have too great a quantity we might wreck the entire underworld. According to my calculations the smallest fragment possess a power of inconceivable violence.'

'The first thing we have to do,' Abna responded, 'is build a projector – a portable one – capable of generating the required supersonic vibration. The projector must be put aboard the Ultra. We must refit and fuel up; then go on a lone journey and test the stuff. We might even try it on the Great Glacier and see if it halts it.'

'Two birds with one stone,' the Amazon agreed. 'A good idea.'

Their plan decided upon, they both set to work, but it was a job which took far longer than they had estimated. With intervals for rest and refreshment, and discussions with Chris Wilson upon the various details connected with shelter life – at which he was informed, to his delight, that the doomed sun might yet be saved – it took three days to complete the projector. Its wavelength was tested by instruments, the atomium being well out of range, and was found to be correct at 3,000,000 vibrations to the second. There remained nothing but to test the stuff in actual practice – so on the fifth day the refuelled Ultra started off once more into the skies.

The Ultra also carried Morris Arnside, of which fact the

Amazon and Abna were unaware. This last surviving member of the former triumvirate had watched the Amazon and Abna assiduously – not because he was interested in their experiments but because he was anxious to stop them. He knew, as did the rest of the shelter population, what was afoot. There was nothing he wanted more than to destroy the Amazon's plans as his own had been. That he was wrecking the hopes of all humanity of the sun's return mattered nothing.

So at this moment, having slipped unnoticed amidst the crowd before the Amazon and Abna had entered the Ultra, he was concealed in the vessel's false roof, peering down into the control room through the ventilator slats. As yet his plan was not ready to be put into action. That would come later.

'The glacier's getting dangerously close,' the Amazon commented presently, nodding through the main window.

Abna looked. The machine, heading swiftly northward at 2,000 feet, through air which was brilliantly clear with frost and a 50-below zero temperature, had come within range of the advancing barrier. It was awe-inspiring, rearing a mile and a half into the air, its deadly crushing maw composed of powdered granite, rock, slag, and all the stony amalgam it had gathered in its ponderous creep from the Arctic Circle.

The Ultra circled high above it. There was no doubt that once that mass closed over the British Isles the entombed survivors would stay below forever until warmth came and melted the ice by natural means. No heat beams would be able to break it open as long as the frigid, interspacial cold remained outside to harden it to iron rigidity. And, when the southerly glacier joined it, then indeed the end of the surface world would be complete – the Earth a dead planet, in its cocoon of frozen air and snow, the few survivors existing below, their future unpredictable, the generations yet to come never to know the meaning of blue sky, soft winds, or the friendly warmth of a golden sun.

Thoughts such as these passed swiftly through the Amazon's mind as she considered the Great Glacier; then she turned to Abna as she slowed the Ultra down.

'What do we do?' she asked him. 'You seem to know more about atomium than I do.'

He responded. 'Halt the Ultra – make it stationary – and then we'll lower a square inch of atomium to the glacier. We'll keep it in the sights of the projector and from a safe distance we'll release the supersonic beam. Then we'll see – and doubtless feel – what happens.'

The Amazon gave a nod and turned to make preparations. The atomium cube, so small as to look ridiculous, was lowered swiftly on the cradle and wire to the white wilderness below. It was a scarcely visible dark speck to the naked eye – but in the sights of the projector which Abna was handling, it came clearly into focus.

'You drive,' he instructed. 'And we'd better use dark goggles. The glare from this stuff is likely to be terrific.'

He handed over a pair of purple goggles, donned a pair himself, and then the Amazon settled at the controls. She circled the machine once or twice, then bringing the helicopter screws into play she set it motionless, hovering a mile from the speck which, though quite invisible to her through the dark glasses, Abna said he could detect clearly through the projector sights.

'Ready?' he questioned.

The girl looked intently through the window. 'Ready – yes.'

The projector hummed and through the freezing air there stabbed the supersonic vibration, in a straight line. What happened afterward the Amazon was not at all sure – nor was Abna, who was more or less expecting it.

Small though the fragment of atomium was, its compressed energy was far beyond anything ever before known. Three square miles of glacier lifted right out of the earth, its granite hardness smashed into powder. In the midst of a chaos of mushrooming smoke and intolerable flame, blinding even through the purple glasses, the atomium exploded. Tremendous air disturbances bounced and rocked the Ultra, swinging it from its hovering position.

The Amazon clung to the controls, operated them swiftly, and rode the tortured air for a while – then gradually the disturbances began to subside, leaving behind a mighty cleft in the glacier, the water within it already freezing over and a towering column of woolly smoke climbing bank upon bank into the icy heaven.

'That,' she exclaimed, tugging off her goggles and looking at Abna eagerly, 'is power! Real power! If we had enough of it we could destroy the glacier completely.'

'We could, but we'd only fight a losing battle,' Abna replied, thinking. 'As fast as we destroyed it it would freeze over again, as that rent is doing now . . . No; we need all the atomium we can get for rekindling the sun and let the glacier take care of itself.'

The Amazon reflected for a moment and then said: 'There's only one thing against that, Abna. To have found the power of atomium is only half the battle without enough of the stuff to carry out our project – and even granting we do find enough of it we've still to work out a master plan by which we can use it to save the sun. Also, once we're below ground in the shelter we'll stay there, helpless, if the glacier covers the shelter before we can put our plan into operation.'

Abna moved to the control board and sat down, considering each problem in turn.

'To find more atomium shouldn't be too difficult,' he said presently. 'In the laboratory at the shelter is the big detector, more sensitive than this one we have in here. With what little atomium we have left completely insulated the detector will show us where the next source of it lies. We collect that, insulate it, and go on to the next source of supply – and so on until we have enough. Obviously the stuff will be in space, so into space we shall have to go to get it.'

'Yes, Abna, but think of the time we'll lose coming back to earth with each lot we find!'

'We won't come back to earth. We need a base where we can dump the stuff as fast as we get it – and it seems to me there is no better spot for that job than Mercury.'

'The nearest planet to the sun, eh?' the Amazon mused. 'Good idea! All right, that settles it – but how do we operate our plan before the glacier covers the shelter?'

'We live here in the Ultra, in space, until our job is done. We have laboratory equipment and we'll be travelling space a good deal in any case – so it is the logical move. If the other people get trapped in the shelter, they can emerge when we have rekindled the sun.'

'My fear,' the Amazon said dubiously, 'is that we'll never find enough of the stuff for our purpose. However, granting we do find enough my suggestion is that we transport it to the sun from Mercury, using the Ultra for the job, of course, cutting the stuff loose from the grapples when it is within the sun's field of attraction.'

She paused, frowning over a thought. Abna looked at her in surprise. 'Perfect so far,' he approved. 'What's bothering you?'

'The fact that the plan is all wrong.'

'But it isn't! That is exactly what we must do.'

The Amazon hurried on: 'I've been basing all my calculations on the fact that atomium would be disintegrated by the internal heat still remaining in the sun; now we know that it won't. Nothing will detonate it except that special supersonic vibration. How do we get around that? It needs atmosphere if it is to function properly, as do all vibrations which come technically into the category of sound.'

'The sun has an atmosphere, Vi – a gaseous envelope. Normally it is flaming gas, but at present it will be air of sorts, sufficient for our purpose to carry the wave-length.'

The Amazon sighed. 'You still haven't grasped my meaning. How do we get near enough to the sun's atmospheric envelope to operate the supersonic equipment without ourselves being engulfed in the atomic explosion which we hope will follow when the sun is rekindled?'

Abna was silent, his lips compressed. Clearly he had not considered this aspect.

'Further,' the girl added, 'the sun still has the same huge gravitational mass as when he is ablaze. You can't play tag with a gravitation like that! I tried it once and only just got away in time.'

'There is only one answer to that, since it is essential the projector operates in the solar atmosphere,' Abna said. 'We must do it by remote control . . . In the course of your career you many a time used a duplicate of yourself, I believe – a synthetic flesh model. Is there anything to stop you doing the same again? That creature, answerable only to your will, can descend to the solar atmosphere in a small space machine which we'll take along attached to the Ultra, and in that machine will be the supersonic projector. Your double, under your orders from Mercury, will release the projector and be destroyed in the doing, perhaps. In any case that doesn't signify as long as the job is done.'

The Amazon's eyes were gleaming. 'Of course! Synthesis never occurred to me while I had my mind on the main problem.'

'Then our next move is to return to London and your underworld lab as fast as possible,' Abna said. 'Move number one is to locate more atomium.'

The Amazon turned to the controls and swung the vessel round on a southward course. Through the slats of the ventilator in the ceiling the gleaming eyes of Morris Arnside watched intently. So far he had heard every word of the conversation and upon whether or not the Amazon and Abna left the Ultra upon landing in London in order to hammer on the doors of the shelter and gain admittance – depended his plan.

Circumstances worked things out exactly as he had hoped. Having no reason to suspect that anybody was aboard the Ultra except themselves the girl and Abna left the machine when they had brought it down within a dozen yards of the shelter doors.

CHAPTER XVIII

Arnside watched them depart, then he slid quickly out of his hiding place, hurried over to the airlock and bolted it. He had studied the Amazon's actions so carefully when she had been at the control panel that he knew enough to be able to set the machine going. The rest he intended to figure out later.

So the only warning the Amazon and Abna received was when they had just reached the shelter doors. There was a sudden scream of wind behind them, which they took at first for an oncoming blizzard – then to their amazement the Ultra swept up from the icefield, hurtled towards the black sky, and was gone in the space of seconds.

Abna lowered his gaze from the sky at last and met the girl's coldly gleaming eyes behind the face mask of her furs.

'Can't do anything now,' she said, through the audiophone. 'I assume somebody must be one jump ahead of us.'

'Only one person could be to that extent – Arnside,' Abna responded.

They did not pursue the subject further at that moment, for the doors slid apart in response to their request for admittance; but once within the shelter and with the doors shut again they exchanged grim glances as they pulled off their furs.

'Something wrong?' asked Chris Wilson, to the forefront of the interested people who had been awaiting the return of the pair and a report on their experiment.

'Where's Arnside?' the Amazon demanded.

'Arnside?' Chris looked puzzled. 'Why, I – Come to think of it, I haven't seen him for the last few hours. Does it matter?'

'He has just stolen the Ultra!'

'You mean he must have smuggled himself aboard?' Ethel asked in amazement.

'That's just what I mean, Rosy.' The Amazon tightened her lips for a moment. 'This serves me right! I should have wiped him out when I had the chance, as I did Torrington and Swainson.'

'Is it such a tragedy him stealing the Ultra?' Chris asked. 'You can build a new machine, can't you? Or for that matter, there is Abna's machine, every bit as useful even if not as big . . . I suppose Arnside's nerve broke or something and he's made a dash into space, where he thinks he can perhaps find safety.'

The Amazon shook her head. 'I wish I could believe that. What worries me is that he heard everything we said – and saw, too. He knows atomium can be exploded with a supersonic wave, and he knows every detail of the plan we've made for rekindling the sun. Aboard that vessel is the supersonic projector we used, but, fortunately, no atomium. If, with the detector, he should discover some more atomium, he could drop it on this shelter, detonate it with the projector beam, and so blow us off the face of the Earth.'

'Why should he want to do that?' Ethel asked blankly. 'He has been so completely on our side since you smashed up the triumvirate—'

'He may have fooled you, but he didn't fool me,' the Amazon interrupted. 'I thought he'd try to pull something some day, but I never expected this! I smashed up his plans to better his future at the expense of other people – and that seems to make it logical that he'll try and smash mine, and thereby also destroy everybody else's chances into the bargain.'

'Whatever he does, or attempts to do, we have our own plans to carry out,' Abna said. 'But for that pressing necessity we could go into space in my machine and try to track him down. We may even find him when we start searching for atomium.'

'We must find him!' the Amazon declared. 'As long as he's at large he'll do everything he can to ruin our plans.'

'Arnside apart,' Ethel said eagerly, 'what happened to the experiment? Did it work, Aunt Vi? Can the sun be revived?'

'I have every reason for thinking so,' the Amazon responded, and there was a roar of delight from the assembly. 'But Abna and I have got to work fast. Our next job is in the laboratory.'

Chris nodded, and the Amazon and Abna wasted no time in hurrying to their scientific retreat.

'What a tragedy it is that the Ultra has that atomium detector aboard,' the Amazon said bitterly, as she switched the large one into commission. 'Arnside may steal every scrap of atomium he can find to stop us getting it.'

Abna said: 'He can't do that. This detector here – which we'll mount in my flyer later – shows us where atomium is. It would lead us straight to it – and maybe Arnside. I don't think he'd be crazy enough to risk that possibility.'

The atomium detector claimed the Amazon's attention. The needle came to rest pointing diagonally above and moving gently. Abna raised his eyes to the girl's.

'In space and on the move,' he said. 'Probably that meteoric lump which hit your coffin-ship. It may be moving in a fixed orbit. See how far away it is.'

The Amazon set to work with the calculating equipment and finally got a figure of 200,000 miles.

'About 40,000 miles short of the moon's orbit,' she said. 'All right, we'll go and find it, and let's hope it's the first of a mass of it which can be dumped on Mercury, Arnside permitting. Your vessel has the necessary magnetic grapples, I suppose?'

'Yes, but remember that we need a small secondary pick-a-back ship to take with us, in which will be that synthetic image of you. We'll also need a new supersonic projector, since our friend has oblingingly flown away with ours.'

'Delay, delay!' the Amazon breathed. 'With every minute counting—' She switched on the visiphone to headquarters, where Chris Wilson was presiding. His face appeared on the screen.

'Yes, Vi? Something I can do?'

'What is the latest bolometer reading of the sun?'

Chris answered: 'At noon today is was 1,600 centigrade and still falling.'

'Whew!' the Amazon whistled, startled. 'It's expiring at a frightening rate. All right, thanks. Send in the chief engineer, will you?'

'Sixteen hundred?' Abna repeated. 'Assuming the rate of decline remains constant, that gives us four weeks in which to revive the sun. After that he'll become a white dwarf. Of course the speed of decline accelerates as the deadline is neared.'

The Amazon declared: 'From the chief engineer I want full co-operation in the building of the pick-a-back space ship; then I have the synthetic model to make while you build a new supersonic projector—'

The Amazon turned as the chief engineer entered the laboratory and came hurrying across to her. She gave him the details and then sat down with him to sketch out the plan of the machine she wanted – a small vessel with nothing more intricate about it than normal radio controls so that radio beams could guide it from the intended base station on Mercury.

'And I want it in 48 hours,' the Amazon told him when at last she had the plans to her satisfaction.

'You'll get it, Miss Brant,' the engineer assured her, 'if I have to press into commission every man and woman in the shelter.'

While Abna went to work to build a new projector – an intricate job even with plenty of time to spare – she set about the task of creating a synthetic image of herself. Abna, in the few moments he could spare, watched her progress. In this particular field of synthetics he admitted that she knew far more than he and it was a confession which made her smile with something of her old superiority.

Synthesis, however, was a process which could not be hurried, and the Amazon fretted and fumed in consequence. Abna did neither. He forced her to rest at intervals, saw that she ate regularly, and helped her wherever he could. First an electric 'patterner' took an impression of her image, both external and internal, which impression was passed on electronically to a shapeless mass of synthetic flesh in a vacuum tube. As a negative might appear in the developing bath, so the flesh assumed the outward appearance of the Golden Amazon, right down to the tiniest scar and exact even to the number of hairs on her head.

'Brilliant, Vi – brilliant,' Abna complimented her, studying the perfect, apparently sleeping form in the sealed tube. 'Though I must say I prefer the original!'

'If you met this image of mine walking about you wouldn't know the difference,' the Amazon said.

'You think not? That is because you cannot see the living

animation in your eyes, the tremendous air of energy that hangs about you. No image could fool me, Vi. I've studied you too closely for that. Am I to understand,' Abna asked, 'that the brain of this image is its main motive power? It doesn't come to life and act on its own?'

'It could, but it doesn't. A radio brain, responsible to my will alone, is what I use. I once did discover how to create life, but . . .' The Amazon stopped, pressing finger and thumb into her eyes. 'That was long ago when I wanted above all else to rule the world. I have learned better sense since then.'

Abna contemplated her broodingly: 'In some ways you are far cleverer than I,' he said at last. 'You can create life and duplicate any living thing. You are the mistress of life, which is the ultimate achievement. We of Atlantis have never solved that problem, so to you belongs the glory.'

'I don't think it is glorious to create life,' the girl replied. 'It is assuming far too much. It's dangerous – terrifying! I never want to attempt it again. Life, like death, is Nature's own responsibility. That secret is one which I shall never divulge, or use again.'

She turned, opened the vacuum tube, and spoke sharply.

'Get up and walk!' she ordered.

The image did so, moving like a somnambulist across the laboratory and halting only when the Amazon so commanded.

'You have the supersonic projector finished?' the Amazon asked, turning back to Abna.

'To the last detail. All we are waiting for now is the pick-a-back ship. Since you said 48 hours that gives us six more hours of freedom. Don't you think we're entitled to leave this laboratory for a while and talk of other things? Let's go into the galleries. The change will do us good.'

She accompanied him from the laboratory, through the headquarters office – where Chris Wilson glanced up briefly from his work – and so out to the main shelter. Here they wandered along one of the countless galleries which, at intervals, had portholes embedded in granite. Through these it was possible to see the outer world, the warmth of the shelter keeping the immensely tough glass free of frost.

'Here,' Abna said, and drew the girl down to a natural seat

in the rock beside one of the portholes. 'I want to talk to you, Vi, not of science, but about you and me. You don't suppose, after the battle we're fighting together, after the association which has sprung up between us, that I ever intend to let you go, do you?'

'Frankly, I'd never thought about it.'

'Then do, while you have a moment. It's important.'

'Well, what can I say?'

'Just three words. They're pretty ordinary, I believe, but you people of Earth – the normal ones I mean – attach a great deal of importance to them.'

The Amazon laughed gently. 'You mean "I love you"?'

'That's it. Do you?' Abna insisted. 'You must surely know from my efforts to reach you that you mean more to me than anything else in the universe—'

He broke off, frowning at the girl's expression. She was staring fixedly through the porthole, fascinated. Startled, he turned and look, too. Then he saw it in all its awe-inspiring majesty—

The Great Glacier was coming.

CHAPTER XIX

Immediately the Amazon was on her feet and Abna jumped up beside her.

'It can't be more than two miles away!' he ejaculated. 'That means that at the rate it's moving it will be over the shelter in something like an hour.'

'We've got to get out quickly!' the Amazon interrupted. 'And if that pick-a-back vessel isn't finished we'll have to go without it.'

She turned and raced to the headquarters office. Chris Wilson looked up in surprise; then his surprise changed to alarm as the Amazon explained what was happening. She snapped on the inter-phone.

'Get the chief engineer here immediately,' she ordered.

'I'll go and see how the shelter's progressing,' Chris said. 'Finished or not we'll have to go below—'

He dashed from the office, and in a few seconds the engineer came hurrying in.

'I know what's the matter, Miss Brant,' he said breathlessly. 'I heard the reports about the glacier. That pick-a-back ship you wanted is finished. I've got men transporting it now to your laboratory.'

'Good!' the Amazon acknowledged. 'See they clamp it on top of Abna's flyer, as arranged. I'll join you later.'

The engineer nodded and hurried out. Swiftly the Amazon followed him, Abna coming up behind her. In the main shelter outside people were milling back and forth, aware of the sudden imminent danger. Then Chris Wilson came hurrying up.

'What about it?' the Amazon asked quickly. 'Is it safe enough for the people to go below?'

He nodded. 'The shelter's finished and the shaft can be sealed off safely. The test will come when that load of ice settles above. If the shelter stands up to it it will be okay. There are only small details to finish, such as drainage, crop planting, and the like.'

'You'll see us when we've revived the sun,' the Amazon told him. 'If we don't suceed this is the last time we'll see each other, I'm afraid.'

There was confidence in Chris' smile as he shook hands with the girl and then with Abna.

'You'll do it between you,' he said – and then dashed away to attend to the details of getting the people below.

The Amazon and Abna raced back through the headquarters office to the laboratory. Beyond it, in the hangar, the chief engineer was supervising the clamping of the pick-a-back machine to the top of Abna's strange craft.

'All in order?' the Amazon inquired, and he nodded.

'Yes. It should be okay, Miss Brant. Everything just as you ordered it.'

'Thanks. You better go and take your men with you. You have just time to get below before the glacier arrives.'

The men departed swiftly. Abna glanced at the Amazon.

'Get your image and put it in this subsidiary machine,' he said. 'I'll check up on all needful things in the vessel.'

He climbed quickly through the airlock and into the craft, and he and the Amazon started to work at top speed. Even so it took them 15 minutes to get all the details straight. Then the Amazon climbed into the machine's control room. As she closed the airlock door Abna switched on the power – that mysterious degravitative power which only seemed to be understood by him.

The men who guarded the doors of the hangar roof set them sliding apart and the ship darted out into the blackness of the afternoon and was gone.

The people moved below to their new quarters, and Chris gave a sigh of relief as, standing in the brilliant cold lights of the vast underground cavern, he watched the massive slide closing into position, sealing the buried city from the upper world, perhaps only until scientific wizardry rekindled the sun.

'Pity we can't see the glacier coming,' Ethel remarked, as with her mother she stood at her father's side.

'I'm thankful we can't,' he responded. 'We'll feel it when it smashes down the upper cavern and the remains of what used to be Charing Cross station.'

Ethel nodded. Perhaps it was a mercy that the x-ray screens, which later would give a view of the outer world through the solid rock and ice, were not yet completed.

'I wonder,' Ethel mused, as she watched the sealing valve close the shaft, 'if the rest of the people surviving in the world have kept themselves safe?'

'Up to a week ago they had,' her father replied. 'We were in touch by radio until then. Most of the big cities have their shelters in all parts of the world.'

A hush fell on the multitude of people who had gathered at the base of the shaft. They just could not bring themselves to move or take up the threads of existence again until they knew what their fate was to be. Most of them motionless, their faces drawn and strained, they stood waiting.

Then the glacier arrived, signalling its approach by a series of concussions from somewhere above as ice-locked buildings were smashed to atoms before the irresistible advance. A slow-moving landslide, over a mile high, pushing everything inexorably before it, the glacier rolled across the space where the shelter lay, and the din of those countless tons of frozen matter on the move was well nigh unbearable below, sending shattering vibratory waves of sound through the rock which stung the eardrums and tortured the nervous system.

The shelter – as must all those throughout the country which had experienced the glacier's arrival – quivered violently as if in the grip of an earthquake. The glacier had become far bigger than before, having accumulated entire mountains on its way, pulverizing them as it travelled. Now the colossal pressure bore down on the shelter and the racked, tortured people within stood their ground as the din increased and the vibration became a terrifying thing that it seemed must bring the metal-lined walls crashing in upon them.

The people began to fall like so many toys, prostrate before the concussive effect of the waves of sound. The buried shelter swayed, the metal walls creaked under the strains – but they did not give way.

Chris Wilson, flat on his back, clinging desperately to consciousness, slowly began to realize that the frightful quaking was subsiding. The glacier was moving on and had left behind its main mass, a mile thick perhaps, with this shelter buried under it – to remain forever sealed unless two scientific brains battling with a cosmic catastrophe could somehow restore chaos to normalcy.

The Amazon and Abna, far out in space, were not permitted to see what happened when the great glacier arrived over London's main shelter, for the glacier brought with it such huge air disturbances that dense clouds hid the scene below from view – a fact which caused a troubled look to settle on the Amazon's features.

'I'd like to have known how they fared,' she muttered, seated with Abna at the control board. 'Do you suppose we might find out by radio?'

'Unlikely. Solar interference for one thing, and the electrical storms generated on the surface by the movement of the glacier for another. Not that I think you have any need to worry. I'm sure the shelter would survive.'

The Amazon, typically, since she could not do anything about the matter, put it on one side for the time being and turned to study the atomium-detector. The needle pointed diagonally upward, roughly in the direction of the pale shadow which was the moon. Beside the detector was another instrument which set the course, its needle lying exactly parallel with the detector finger.

'I wonder what happened to Arnside,' the Amazon mused, looking through the telescopic sights. 'I don't see him anywhere, and I certainly don't think he'd ever have the nerve to fly to the outer solar system. He must be lingering somewhere, waiting to spring something.'

'We can deal with him if he does,' Abna responded. 'I have weapons on this vessel which are even more deadly than those on your Ultra. Some of them can even work through the fourth dimension, by which a straight beam can be made to turn a corner – or so it appears.'

Abna studied the instruments for a while, made some calculations, and then said:

'At our present speed we should reach the area where the atomium is located in something like two hours. In the meantime I'd like to take up our conversation from where it was interrupted by the arrival of the glacier.'

The Amazon did not look at him. She kept her eyes to the telescopic sights. 'About me, you mean?' she asked.

'Yes. When all this is over, Vi – when we have restored the sun, if we can – what do you suppose we are going to do? You surely don't intend that you will continue your scientific experiments back on Earth and that I will go back to my people on Jupiter?'

'Why not?' she asked. 'There is always something to be learned. You are aware of that yourself. You do not understand synthesis of life. I do not understand the fourth dimension. Those two subjects alone are worth a lifetime's study, are they not?'

'Perhaps, but I have the feeling that a woman of your turn of mind is seeking something far more satisfying than the mysteries of the fourth dimension. You are not a dabbler, Vi, playing with this experiment and then that; there must be some purpose behind the work you do.'

'Yes, there is,' she admitted. 'Call it a dream, if you like, but at least I have made part of it come true. I am trying, planet by planet – excluding Mercury so near to the sun, and Pluto so far away – to create a union of the Solar System, to bring all the planets together under one government – a sane, sensible government. To that end I have brought the moon under Earth's jurisdiction; then came Venus after a good deal of trouble, and then Mars – which led to the present solar disaster when I flung the remainder of the Martian race, bent on ruthless invasion of Earth, into the sun.'

'If the sun recovers, then, and you continue with your plan, Jupiter will come next,' Abna pointed out. 'He's the next world in order from the sun – the first of the outer planets.'

CHAPTER XX

The Amazon smiled. 'Yes, I had intended Jupiter to be next for colonization. Now that can never be. You and your race will never consent to being controlled by a universal government which has its headquarters on Earth and me at the head.'

'You!' Abna looked surprised. 'So far you haven't tried to rule the Earth. Do you mean that you intend to?'

'If the sun recovers, yes. Up to now I have always allowed government to be handled by others – but they have never ruled with a great deal of sense, and I also believe it is a mistake to have different countries with different governments. It destroys all chance of unity because of opposing ideologies – so henceforth I shall personally rule, and I am convinced that if I bring the sun back the people of Earth will want me as their leader, which is something I have always hoped for since that long gone day when I was outcast for trying to rule the world by force.'

'There is one way in which Jupiter can come into your plan,' Abna said. 'By your uniting with – that is marrying – me.'

The Amazon gazed broodingly out of the window on to the depthless majesty of space and the dying sun.

'Why not?' Abna persisted. 'We are two of a kind – both scientific, both young in physique. We each have a different science; we each understand something the other does not. Together we could pool our knowledge and the United Solar System would be infinitely nearer being realized. Remember there are other worlds you still have to master after Jupiter – Uranus, Saturn, and Neptune. What they contain we don't know because we have been at no pain to find out.'

'No man ever talked to me like this before,' the Amazon said.

'Probably no man had cause to as I have.'

For a long time the Amazon was silent; then she said: 'Suppose we talk of this again when we have less on our minds?'

'But surely you can say whether or not you have any regard for me?'

'I admire your scientific prowess, Abna.' The Amazon's violet eyes contemplated him frankly, a vague, half-puzzled light in their depths. 'And as a man you leave little to be desired. As for love – it is only an emotion, and a rather foolish one. No union is based on love; it is physical attraction every time.'

Abna sighed and gave a slight smile. 'All right, we'll discuss it again later,' he agreed.

The Amazon turned back to the telescopic sights. There was no sign of the Ultra. Then as time passed she gave up looking for the vanished Arnside and concentrated with Abna upon the task of locating the mass of atomium which the detector showed existed.

They came within range of it unexpectedly when they had reached 200,000 miles from Earth. It was moving swiftly away from them following an erratic orbit in its soundless sweep through the void.

'That's it!' the Amazon cried, pointing through the window. 'Whether it's the same chunk which hit me when I was in the rocket ship I don't know, but it's certainly possible— And the size of it!' she went on eagerly. 'There's enough power there to blow a couple of planets into dust!'

'From the look of things it's following an orbit round the moon,' Abna said, studying the mass. 'Our job is to grab it and take it to Mercury, then see how much more of it we can find.'

While he controlled the vessel, swinging it in close to the enormous grey mass, the Amazon handled the magnetic grapples, finally anchoring the stuff and tailing it along in their wake as Abna headed in the direction of Mercury. He could only lay his course by calculations since the planet itself, due to the feeble light of the dying sun, was not even visible.

'I suppose,' the Amazon said, looking through the rear port upon the trailing atomium, 'that we haven't enough here for our purpose?'

'I doubt it. The sun's area is tremendous. I estimate that we'll need twice as much to get an effectual core of energy.'

'You'd better insulate this stuff, Abna, so it doesn't affect the detector needle.'

He got up. 'All right. Take over for a while.'

The Amazon did not particularly like having to admit that neutralizing the atomium's attraction was something she did not understand. She watched silently as he switched on one of his instruments which, he explained, generated an insulative shield round the stuff and prevented it affecting the detector. The Amazon glanced at it. The needle was now pointing straight ahead instead of to the rear.

'More atomium somewhere, right in our track,' she commented. 'All the better.'

Abna returned to the control board, leaving his neutralizing radiation in operation. The Amazon went to the window again. For a few seconds she caught a glimpse of what appeared to be showers of stars, clearly discernable against the moon's rocky, deserted face.

'The Ultra!' she ejaculated. 'Exhaust from the firing tubes! That's what that was!'

Abna turned and looked at her sharply. 'Where?'

'On the moon, just a moment ago. That's where Arnside must have been hiding. He's probably kept track of our movements with the telescope ever since we left Earth. Now, although we can't see him at the moment, I take it that he's following us.'

She hurried across to the telescopic sights and swung them through a wide arc, studying the void intently; but it was impossible to see the Ultra against the star-dusted backdrop. In normal circumstances the glare of the sun would have picked the vessel out as a silver pencil, but the present exhausted red glow failed to provide the least tell-tale reflection, and since he was in space moving at a fixed velocity Arnside had no further use for the rocket tubes either, so their exhaust did not give away his position.

'Thank heaven there's no air,' the Amazon muttered, giving up her scrutiny of the void. 'If there were he could detonate this stuff we're dragging along and that would be the end of us.'

'And him,' Abna pointed out. 'The blast from a chunk as big as that would blow him to powder even at 500 miles – and the projector certainly cannot operate over that range. No need to worry on that score. He must have something else in mind.'

The Amazon said nothing. She sat down and began to make calculations.

'On Mercury,' the girl said at length, looking up, 'there is likely to be a very thin atmosphere. Air of sorts. Normally when the sun is at his natural glory there is no air on Mercury. But now, with the sun's heat no more than a glimmer, that atmosphere will have spread uniformly over the planet. It should be a temperate planet on the sunward side. And if there is air Arnside can detonate the atomium once we're within atmosphere. That he will destroy himself as well doesn't concern him, I think I'm convinced that his aim is to wipe us out, no matter what the cost to himself?'

Abna shrugged. 'We'll have to risk it, that's all. What we can do is put on speed to such an extent that we'll outdistance him, and he may lose us.'

He operated the controls, building speed upon speed, until presently the velocity became so tremendous that both he and the girl, in spite of their superhuman constitutions, began to feel the strain.

'We're going to move a lot faster yet,' Abna said, turning a drawn face to the girl, 'but it will be more than we can take sitting like this. I'll have to set the course and let the machine carry on on its own until it achieves a constant velocity. Then we'll be able to move again. One thing is certain – Arnside won't be able to keep pace with this!'

He snapped in the automatic controls, then got up and motioned the softly-sprung wall couches. He settled on one, lying flat out on his back; and the Amazon on the other – but whereas he gave himself up to the drifting unconsciousness occasioned by the stupendous pressure of acceleration, the Amazon remained with her wits about her, controlling her breathing, throwing no extra strain on her heart. She was accustomed to such ordeals as this, and hardened to them. Every muscle and nerve was under discipline. Unconsciousness would only come if she relaxed.

For a long time she lay thinking, staring at the roof of the control room; then in the shadowless light her eyes moved to consider the young giant stretched senseless a couple of yards away from her.

The Amazon preferred to test everything minutely before she accepted it. There was only one way to be sure of Abna, and that was to read his innermost thoughts. So far, the Amazon had never had the opportunity. He was unconscious, his mind uncontrolled, and she had the gift of reading thoughts by exerting her extraordinary mentality to the full.

So she concentrated, gazing at him fixedly. With no calls upon her physique, she could give her mental power full play, and gradually she found herself in tune with the Atlantean giant's thoughts. She examined them in detail with her usual mathematical precision. She saw that much he had said about his race and Jupiter, and the Great Red Spot had been true – but she also saw something else which he had never mentioned.

It left her with a cold glint in her eyes and a tautness about her mouth. When she had finished concentrating she no longer wondered what answer she would give to Abna when the issue between them arose again.

CHAPTER XXI

When the ship had travelled far beyond the orbit of Venus and was still hurtling with incredible velocity toward Mercury, the required constant speed was achieved and the strangling pull of acceleration ceased. The Amazon got up from the couch and went to the outlook window.

The vessel had almost completed the tremendous trip. The sun filled all the void, a titanic globe of deep red, his photosphere a mass of black fissures. He was not eye-shattering to look upon; no appreciable heat radiated from his gigantic bulk. Away to the right, in the accustomed spot, hung Mercury, a thin pink ring of atmosphere round his globe. The Amazon gave a grim smile as she realized that her calculation concerning air had been accurate. Where Mercury had never been able to retain a proper atmosphere envelope in normal times, he now had one when it was too late. When – or if – the sun became a white dwarf the air would freeze solid.

'Where do you suppose that atomium is, Vi?' Abna asked. 'The detector needle is still pointing ahead.'

Frowning, she went to the instrument, tested it, but found it working perfectly.

'The atomium is still a million miles distant,' Abna said. 'I can think of only one answer, incredible though it is . . . Mercury himself is atomium, a whole planet of it!'

The Amazon gazed out for a while upon the small, dizzy little planet.

'Yes, why not?' she breathed at last. 'For untold ages, ever since the birth of the solar system. Mercury has been soaked in the radiation of the sun, always circling dangerously near to him. What more likely than that Mercury has been a kind of cosmic sponge, soaking up the vast sluices of energy the sun has poured forth, until Mercury has himself become a mass of crystallized energy? Great heavens! If only we could throw Mercury in the sun and then detonate him!'

Abna shook his head, looking up from the calculations he

had been making on the control bench beside him.

'It wouldn't be practical. For one thing we haven't enough power to shift an entire planet, even though he is only small; and for another we'd have too much atomium. Instead of re-kindling the sun we'd probably blow him in pieces!'

'I see. Well, at least we have atomium enough for our purpose. All we have to do is land on Mercury, hack off as much of the stuff as we need, and then carry it sunward.'

'Correct,' Abna agreed. 'And what we have to do is find out how much we need. Help me calculate.'

The Amazon settled beside him, and between them, aided by the mathematical machines, they worked out how much material they wanted. By the time they had finished, Mercury was looming dangerously close. Abna turned to the controls, slowed the vessel up and then brought it down with scarcely a jar on the sunward side of the little planet.

Abna was silent, considering the scene with her. They had dropped in a cup-shaped depression, the curious rippled formation of the ground showing how furious heat had subsided into a solid plasma, leaving the marks of ebb and flux behind. To the right was a low barrier range of mountains and over them in an almost black, star-dusted sky the sun loomed, his mighty caverned face roughly bisected by the saw-teeth of the range.

'Journey's end,' the Amazon said at length. 'And I wonder what happened to Arnside. Do you suppose we lost him?'

'We certainly outdistanced him,' Abna got up from a bolometer reading of the sun's atmosphere. 'Eight hundred degrees,' he said. 'A few more below and he'll be over the deadline. We've got to act fast.'

The Amazon nodded and together they turned to the apparatus. Since they had an entire mountain range nearby to work on, they directed disintegrator beams upon it, hacking vast pieces of the coke-like, immensely heavy material and then gathering them up with the magnetic grapple. The task was easy. The light gravity of the plane's mass made the cutting and hacking simple, and the dragging work too. All the Amazon and Abna had to do was sit and watch as they controlled the apparatus.

At the end of two hours they had at the rear of the ship a mighty pile of the rockery. Abna switched off the disintegrator and turned to another instrument. Its reading gave him the exact mass of the material obtained.

'Thirty-seven hundred,' he said finally. 'We planned we needed 3,600, so this is just about right. A bit one way or the other doesn't signify. We're all ready to make the experiment. As near as I can judge, we will have to make three trips.'

Abna settled himself at the control board, switched in the strange degravitive devices, and his machine swept into the void, the mass of atomium in the grip of the magnetic grapples at the rear.

Within a few minutes the slight pull of Mercury had been shaken loose and the enormous tagging strain of the sun made itself felt. At close quarters his dying face was an incredible sight to gaze upon. He was not so much like a sun, a blinding cauldron of unthinkable raging energies, as a gigantic Mars, his redly flickering surface corroding with the areas of darkness. Even so heat existed sufficiently to kill human life, if it came too close, and against this Abna took every precaution.

Gradually turning his vessel, he waited until he was flying diagonal to the sun, then he gave the Amazon the signal. She opened the switch which controlled the magnetic grapples and the atomium was cast loose. It began flying through space in a huge, mountainous lump, becoming smaller and smaller, a mere speck against the red vastness, until it was lost to sight.

'Two more trips before we're through,' Abna said.

The Amazon, looking at the sun, nodded – and without any apparent effort against the enormous gravitational drag, Abna made the return trip to Mercury. So finally all the required material had been dumped in the fast cooling mass of the lord of the day – pure crystallized energy, thousands of tons of it, which would sink to the centre of the sun's still gaseous interior and there be held at the centre of gravity. Mathematically, the force of the supersonic wave operating through the solar atmosphere to the interior would detonate the material, and the rest remained to be seen. Figures had said that it must work, but in dealing with cosmic forces there was always the chance of error.

'Now back to Mercury,' the Amazon said, when the final trip was over. 'From there I can control my twin while she operates the supersonic projector from her vessel. I shall see through her eyes exactly what she is doing, feel through her nerves just what her movements are, hear through her ears whatever sounds there may be.'

'In fact, an affinity of the 'nth degree,' Abna smiled.

He turned the machine about and once more the trip back to Mercury was made. It was as they were almost touching down to their valley headquarters, however, that the Amazon stared hard through the window and then gripped Abna's arm.

'Arnside,' she breathed. 'There, in the Ultra, just clear of that mountain range—'

Abna looked, his jaws setting. 'Arnside it is! And if he touches off any part of Mercury with that supersonic projector which is aboard he'll blow us, himself, and half the solar system into the fourth dimension!'

Apparently Arnside had seen them, and he had also gained a good deal of skill in the art of manoeuvre, to judge from the way he handled the Ultra. The big machine swept through the gulf and Abna took a sideways turn to avoid the onrush. Then as he hurtled past, Arnside released a battery of disintegrator beams. Pieces flicked off Abna's machine, but no vital damage appeared to have been done.

'Give it him back, Vi!' Abna snapped. 'Everything we've got! I'll have to control the machine. I understand it better than you.'

The Amazon needed no instructions. She was already at the control board, handling the weapons, sighting the speeding Ultra in the screens. Then she pressed the switches and buttons and hurled a stream of neutronic energy at the vessel. Nothing happened – much to her amazement. There was a flare of light, but the Ultra was otherwise unmarked.

'Of course!' she ejaculated suddenly. 'You sheathed it in that special metal – the same stuff with which we built the shelters. It's proof against neutrons, pressure, heat, and everything else – unless you can spring some four-dimensional tricks?'

Abna shook his head. 'I could, but they wouldn't be any use against that invulnerable metal.'

Watching intently he still kept his craft zig-zagging; then he added. 'I'm not risking descending to Mercury until he is taken care of. If he turns supersonic power on that planet it will be the end of everything. Our one hope is that he does not know Mercury is pure atomium.'

'There's also another hope,' the Amazon responded, watching the Ultra's wild plunging as Arnside did his utmost to get his weapon trained on his objective. 'If you can draw us over the top of the Ultra I could change to it from this machine through the floor trap. Arnside wouldn't be able to do anything to us because he'd be unable to get at us with his weapons. And on top of the Ultra there's an exterior valve I can get through. I'm the only one who knows about it since I built it. Once that's done I can very soon take care of the rest.'

Abna did not hesitate. Abruptly changing his tactics he turned about, to the obvious confusion of Arnside within the Ultra, and then shot up in a vertical ascent. By means of long, sweeping evasive movements he came gradually to a point where he was over the top of the Ultra; then he began to lower his machine foot by foot while the Amazon hastily donned a space suit.

Her only weapon a protron gun, clenched in her gloved hand, she yanked up the floor trap and dropped into the cavity below. Here she was in darkness with the second outer trap closed. In a moment she had it open – the top flap closing automatically to seal in the control room air – to find the Ultra's plates no more than three feet below her in the void.

Easing herself through the hole she forced herself down, the only way she could make the change against the vagaries of gravitation. The instant she touched the Ultra's plates she grabbed the projection tightly and held on, Abna's machine remaining above her.

This was not the first time she had been on the outside of a machine in space – but its effect on her was just the same. It was an unpleasant two-ways-at-once feeling, the various gravities from the two ships, the sun, and Mercury pulling at her body and creating a terrifying elongating feeling. She felt sick for a while, the void all around her – infinite space and depth upon depth. Then she forced herself to concentrate on the only solid thing – the Ultra.

Crawling along its plates she came to the valve she was seeking. A movement of the outer combination lock opened it and she dropped silently into the dark space below which belonged to the false roof.

So far so good. She closed the trap, took off her helmet, and lay breathing hard for a while as she recovered her steadiness. Then she began to creep forward, making no sound, knowing every inch of the course she was taking. So presently she came to the grating which marked the ventilator from the control room. Peering through the slats she beheld Arnside crouched at the control board, staring hard through the outlook window, obviously trying to imagine what had become of Abna's flyer. To one side of him was the control board for the weapons and to the other the navigational instruments.

With one movement the Amazon swept up the ventilator grid and swept down, her right arm circling and gripping under Arnside's chin before he had the chance to turn in his chair. Pinned with that soft but incredibly powerful forearm under his chin he struggled savagely as his hands were dragged away from the switches by the backward movement of his body.

'Now, my friend, I think we have a little score to settle,' the Amazon murmured. 'I warned you what would happen if you didn't play the game straight when I gave you the chance to go on living . . .'

With a sudden tremendous wrench Arnside tore free and struggled out of the control chair. He dived for his gun on the bench, but the Amazon's gloved fist came up into his face and sent him tottering backwards. He hit the wall of the control room, shook his head dazedly, and then stared at her. Her proton-gun was levelled upon him.

'I'd like to kill you in my own way, Arnside, for the trouble you have caused,' she said deliberately; 'but I have too many other things to do. So I'll make it short.'

She fired and the withered corpse of Arnside dropped to the deck.

With a sniff of contempt the Amazon dropped her gun on

the bench, then she snapped on the space radio. Since Abna was only immediately above her he received her message clearly without solar interference.

'Cast off and land on Mercury,' she said. 'I'll bring the Ultra down. You don't have to worry about Arnside any more; he's been taken care of.'

'See you later,' Abna responded.

The Amazon switched off and then settled at the controls. In a moment or two she saw Abna's machine head for Mercury. She followed at a more leisurely pace, thinking as she went. After a while she smiled tautly and nodded to herself.

'Yes, that should do it,' she murmured, confirming some inner idea.

CHAPTER XXII

She brought the Ultra down on the other side of the mountain range some two miles from the spot where lay the little depression where Abna had descended. Fastening her helmet back in place, she opened the airlock, threw Arnside's dead body to the rocks outside and then began the journey on foot which would bring her to Abna. To do it she had to move through a fairly high cleft which finally brought her within sight of Abna's machine, the pick-a-back space flyer still fastened to its top.

When she came to within a few yards of the airlock Abna opened it and helped her into the control room. He gave a puzzled look as she took off her helmet.

'Why didn't you land the Ultra here?' he asked in surprise. 'It would have saved a lot of time, wouldn't it?'

'I wasn't taking any risk of a collision,' she replied. Then before Abna could comment she added: 'Well, it's time we started the final move, isn't it? My image to detonate the stuff in the sun?'

'From here on it's my party,' she said, wriggling out of her space suit, 'since I am the only one who can control the image.'

'Correct,' Abna agreed. 'Let's get the final details right. – By radio you set the pick-a-back machine off and guide it to the edge of the solar atmosphere. Then by radio amplification you transmit your commands to your image. She then operates the supersonic projector upon the sun, which should detonate the atomium. If she is lost in the doing it will not matter – but if you can save her for some future task all the better.'

'The programme exactly,' the Amazon agreed. 'Here we go.'

She switched on the radio apparatus, able to tell by the dials and indicators exactly what was happening to the pick-a-back spaceship – and sure enough it presently became visible through the ports, heading sunward. From here, however, the sun itself was not visible in his entirety – only half his orb loomed over the mountain range.

The Amazon glanced up. 'Abna, you'd better get into a

space-suit and go to some spot near here were you can see all the sun without difficulty. You'll need the space-suit since the air is too tenuous to breathe. We have got to know exactly what happens and I can't leave these controls, nor can we move this vessel in case I lose the wave length.'

'I'll find a convenient spot somewhere,' Abna responded, taking one of the space suits from the locker and getting into it. Just before he screwed on the helmet and peered experimentally through a pair of purple goggles, the Amazon added:

'There's a good spot to the north-east of the range where you'll get a clear view. I noticed it as I came from the Ultra.'

'Right— And the moment anything starts happening I'll be back.'

'Don't come until you are sure a genuine solar rebirth has set in,' the Amazon advised. 'We're not going to leave things half done.'

Abna put his helmet in position and departed. He kept his eyes on the mighty red ball of the fading sun as he moved. He was a solitary figure in the grey expanse heading toward the mountain range. When he reached it he paused, looking for a good position then remembering the Amazon's suggestion to head north-east he went that way – and came presently to a clear, level track of land which dropped away at the absurdly near horizon. But here indeed was the view he wanted, with all the sun filling the wastes of the void.

He contemplated the titanic orb as he settled down on a rock. He was, he realized, taking a tremendous risk. If the released power of atomium blasted itself forth in one terrific effulgence of energy there was the chance that the sun itself would be blown in pieces and he obliterated before he could move a dozen yards. If, however – as culculation had shown – the energy dissipated itself more or less uniformly then he would behold a sight such as had never been seen before – the gradual restoration of a dying star to its former glory. If this came about he would have ample time in which to return to the flyer before the heat became so intense that the very landscape began to melt and flow as it had done for time immeasurable before the sun had cooled.

He was not sure how long he waited. Time did not seem

to signify just as long as a result was forthcoming. Back in the vessel he pictured the Amazon concentrating on the radio and thought-amplifying beam – and out in space, somewhere between him and the huge red globe was the invisible pick-a-back machine which carried the last hope of restoring the doomed monarch. Abna was even commencing to wonder if, after all, the whole gigantic scientific gamble was proving a failure – when he caught sight of a dim white glow amidst the redness of the centre of the sun.

He had hardly noticed it before it grew brighter and larger. Instantly he slipped on his dark goggles, and only just in time for in complete soundlessness, since there was no air to carry the noise of the unthinkable explosion across the gap, the whiteness flushed across the entire globe. What incredible devouring energies were released at that moment he could only imagine.

Stupendous power was flashing to all parts of the sun, rebuilding the steady atomic processes which had been progressively breaking down. Terrific heat was kindling, building up the fallen temperature. Gases, free electrons, neutrons – all of them were in a state of titanic flux, boiling, scattering, exploding, energy mounting upon energy . . .

Light, blinding even through the goggles, blazed down on Abna as the sun's face became steeped in blinding glare. Heat shafted through the void and he felt it through his space suit. He could look no more upon the risen giant of the day. He had one last glimpse of a vast corona coming into being, together with the twirling prominences of newborn solar life, then he turned and stumbled away, his shadow cut deep on the smoking ground.

His emotions were a curious mixture of exultation and fear. On the one hand the mighty experiment had succeeded and life had been given back to the sun – a life which would continue indefinitely through normal sub-atomic disintegrative process; and on the other hand he wondered if the savage heat would turn the sunward side of Mercury into a molten quagmire before he could reach the vessel where the Amazon was waiting. If his space suit became punctured by any means he was doomed.

It took him three hours to cover the distance – three times as long as his outward journey. Thankfully he stumbled into the control room and slammed the airlock. The Amazon glanced round from the radio board, then got on her feet, her eyes glowing.

'Abna, we made it! We did it! Look at that sun—!' She narrowed her eyes, at the searing half circle visible above the mountain peaks.

'Yes, we made it!' Abna gripped her shoulders thankfully for a moment and then began to get out of his space suit. He asked: 'I suppose that we now head for Earth and see the result of all this?'

The girl shook her head. 'There is no need. As the glaciers melt there'll be the greatest flood since Biblical times. All we would be able to do would be float on the waters like a super-modern ark until they subsided. I think there is a better plan, Abna, now our job is done.'

'You mean?' There was an eager light in Abna's red-blue eyes. 'You mean that you and I—? You're giving me your answer?'

'Yes.' The Amazon considered him frankly. 'For the time being let us go to your planet and rest a while. I'd like to meet your father and the rest of your race. We'll go in this machine, of course; the Ultra will be submerged in molton metal by now.'

'All right, Vi, but before we start do you promise me that—'

'Of course I promise you! I wouldn't come with you otherwise.' The Amazon turned to the wall couch, settled upon it and relaxed. 'While you get the journey started I'm going to rest,' she said, stifling a yawn. 'Controlling that image of mine was no easy job.'

Abna smiled as he settled at the control board. 'Do that. You've earned it.'

He set the ship moving and the girl closed her eyes. Swiftly the machine climbed above the melting plain – then turning away from the savagely brilliant orb of day the vessel plunged into the outer deeps.

Hour followed hour. Abna caught himself dozing at times, in spite of the control he had over himself. The Amazon still slept peacefully. He considered her, smiled to himself, and checked the course . . .

In six hours, moving at its tremendous velocity, the vessel was beyond the orbits of the inner planets with Earth far to the right, black patches showing on the white surface where the sun was melting the mighty ice fields and glaciers. Ahead, already looming larger, was Jupiter.

Abna stirred from a long contemplation of his home planet and moved to the girl's side. He shook her gently.

'Vi, you've been asleep for over six hours. Take a look at Earth – and the world to which we're going—'

The girl did not move. A frown notched Abna's eyebrows for a moment; then he shook her again, more forcibly. This time she stirred lazily and opened her eyes. There was an expressionless, blank look in them which momentarily startled him.

'Take a look—' he began, but the girl cut him short, speaking mechanically.

'I don't need to take a look at Earth, Abna, I am already upon it, floating on the ocean in the Ultra, while you are speeding home!'

'You're what!' Abna jerked the words out and stared at her in dazed wonder.

'Abna,' the girl on the couch said quietly, 'you are not looking at Vi the living but Vi the image. I'm sorry I had to do this to you. Let me explain what happened. I purposely sent you to look at the sun, knowing how you would be delayed in getting back. I was careful not to allow my image to be destroyed once she had done her job. I withdrew her in the pick-a-back machine, knowing you would be too fully occupied to notice the flyer returning to Mercury. I then made her take my place in your vessel. Once that was done I left in a space suit and went to where I had left the Ultra. From the Ultra I controlled her. When I saw you depart – you thinking my image was me – I left in the Ultra for home. And that is where I am now.'

'But why? Why?' Abna shouted, harshness in his voice as he glared down at the lifeless image repeating thought-impulses from faraway Earth.

'Why? Because you lied to me, Abna! You professed to love me. You said you had pursued me because I was the only woman who really mattered to you. One day, all unknown to you, I read your mind, and in it I saw the truth. You wanted union with me because in your race there is not a single surviving female! You believed that I could be forced into marriage with you once we reached your world – and had I not had that glimpse of the truth maybe that would have come about. Now I know why you were so interested in my synthetic life experiment, why you were so regretful that I had decided against using my knowledge in that direction . . . Your race will die out unless you can either find synthesis or a wife. But that wife will not be me.'

Abna was silent, bemused, his fists clenched.

'Perhaps I have made an enemy of you, Abna,' the image resumed. 'Perhaps you will come to Earth to wreak vengeance for my tricking you. Be that as it may. I did think I had found a man at last who was less deceitful than the rest – but in the end I have found you to be more so. You may try to steal other women from Earth – the only planet worth your attention as far as living beings are concerned – but you will not succeed while I watch over their destiny. I have always chosen my own way, and after what has happened I shall continue to do so. The pity is that a man of your great gifts should not know what real love is. All that you said, all that you did, was simply to gain your own ends.'

The image ceased talking for a while, and then added:

'My science against yours, Abna, if it has to be – the modern Earth against the genius of lost Atlantis. It is up to you whether it shall be that.'

There was silence. Abna stared down through the porthole of his machine upon the distant Earth. Somewhere upon it the Ultra was floating, the Amazon within it, her thoughts transmitted over the gulf. For a long time Abna hesitated over the idea of going to Earth and demanding a showdown – then he turned, the bitter glint of defeat in his fine eyes.

He checked the course again for Jupiter, at his side the dead image of the woman who had outwitted him.